CLoy.

◆ THE MAGNET BOOK OF ◆
STRANGE TALES

EDITED BY JEAN RUSSELL

These fourteen strange tales were written specially for this collection by some expert story-tellers. They don't all have ghosts, but each has something weird and inexplicable, taking one step outside reality. Some are macabre, some rather sad, and others have a strangely comic feeling – they will all stretch the imagination and make you wonder.

Who is the pale, skinny boy with old-fashioned roller-skates? Why does Tessie refuse to go upstairs? And what *did* happen to the train full of sheep that went into a tunnel and never came out...?

D1340953

THE MAGNET BOOK OF
STRANGE TALES

EDITED BY JEAN RUSSELL

Illustrated by Tony Ross

A Magnet Book

First published in Great Britain 1980 by Methuen Children's Books Ltd
as *The Methuen Book of Strange Tales*
Magnet paperback edition first published 1981
by Methuen Children's Books Ltd, 11 New Fetter Lane, London EC4P 4EE
Reprinted 1982 and 1985
This volume copyright © 1980 Methuen Children's Books Ltd
Illustrations copyright © 1980 Methuen Children's Books Ltd
She was afraid of upstairs copyright © 1980 Joan Aiken Enterprises Ltd
Printed in Great Britain by Richard Clay (The Chaucer Press) Ltd,
Bungay, Suffolk

ISBN 0 416 21190 9

Contents

Moths

I have always detested moths; especially those big ones that fly through open windows, attracted by a lamp. It has something to do with the way they blunder about a room, leaving powdery smears on the surfaces they collide with; and with those fat bodies that split when swatted, oozing disgusting yellow stuff on to the window.

I suppose most people have something like that: a secret fear or loathing which they keep to themselves because others might laugh or think them cowardly. And I suppose each comes to terms with his weakness one way or another: perhaps by avoiding the hated object, or by learning to accept its appearance with outward calm, at least in company.

My own case is different. By that I don't mean that I have failed to come to terms with my affliction: indeed it might be argued that I have gone too far in the other direction. I mean that the way in which I was *brought* to terms is unique; at least I hope it is. But let me begin, as they say, at the beginning.

It was a hot night; one of those brooding, sticky ones you sometimes get in August when people say what we need is a good thunderstorm and it feels as though we're in for one.

I had a vacation job in the local supermarket; unloading boxes of tinned beans and bottled sauce from wagons and stacking them ceiling-high in the warehouse. It was heavy, hectic work of the sort I might normally have welcomed, because I spent too much time at college sitting about and I like to keep myself in shape. The trouble was, it was too hot. Anyway, after the lunch-break I started feeling sick, and by the time we knocked off at half past five I had a splitting headache so I went home and straight to my room. I opened the window, and lay down on my bed without undressing. I must have slept, because when I next became aware of my surroundings it was dark. I tried to see the time but my wrist-watch is not luminous and I had to turn on the reading-lamp.

My head ached abominably. Squinting at my watch I saw that it was a quarter to ten. I lay back on the pillow. The curtain stirred, and I felt a breath of warm wind on my face. I remember thinking that perhaps the storm we needed was coming. After that there is only a confused blur, out of which shine two recognizable images. One is the bat-packets and the other is the moth.

The bat-packets had breakfast cereal in them. On the back of each was a cut-out picture of a big red bat, with dotted lines that showed you where to cut. If you did this carefully, and fastened the result to a piece of string, you would have a bat that flew round and round your head, whistling. There was a big promotion on, and the supermarket was full of bat-packets.

The moth came in through the window. I ought either to have shut it or turned off the lamp but I did neither and suddenly it was there, looping round and round the light; battering the shade with its dusty paper wings. The bats were off the packets at once, swooping in the yellow glow, round and round with their mouths open. Their whistling filled the room. I cried out to them and they turned on me. The moth was there too – a furry blur; darting in to collide with my face time and time again; trying to get into my mouth. I wrapped my arms around my head and compressed my lips, but the dust was too fine from the moth's wings and I was breathing it in through my nose. I held my breath and the bed began turning, faster and faster. Red bats, two-dimensional, whistled by my head. The moth was forcing its way through the crack between my arms. Its wings were holding it back. It shed them and came on.

I could feel its hard little body, burrowing in towards my face and I pressed my arms together as tightly as I could but still it came. Its antennae tickled my upper lip and it scrabbled there with its fore-legs; pulling its body like a liquorice-torpedo out from between my arms.

I was spinning very rapidly now, and knew that I must breathe, or die. My nostrils were clogged with moth-dust. I opened my mouth a slit, sucking at the air, and felt the little body in my lips: warm custard in a flimsy velvet sac. I retched, spitting; unable to dislodge it. There was a blackness at the back of my head into which I was sinking. It welled up, washing in over my eyes, bearing me away.

I came to in total darkness. It was warm, and there was a strong,

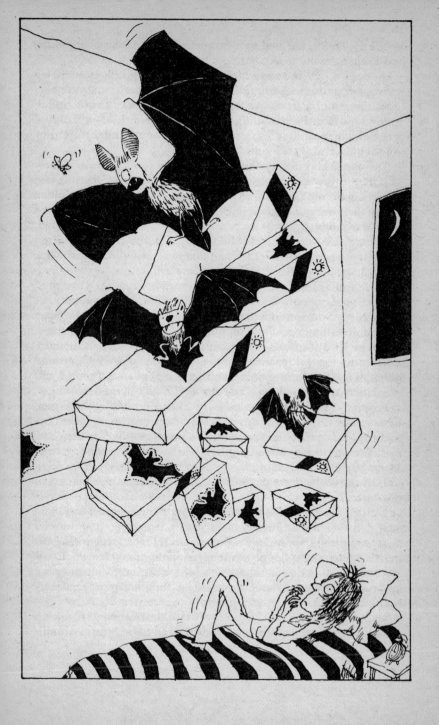

peculiar odour. I seemed to be at rest, and yet I was aware of the most odd sensations in my limbs. My arms, so far as I could tell, were folded on my chest but when I moved them they felt restrained, and at the same time I had the impression that my fingers were enormously long. My legs felt tense, the toes curled under, gripping; I had the notion that if I relaxed them I would fall. For some reason the idea of a strait jacket flashed across my mind. I grew cold with dread. I had gone mad.

The moth. I remembered the moth and explored the inside of my mouth with my tongue. Nothing. I had imagined it, then. It had been in my mind, and so had the red bats. Paper bats that came to life and whirled about my room. Madness. I had been seized with a bout of insanity. That headache was the start of it. I had screamed, thrashing about on my bed. My parents had found me raving and had telephoned for help. They had taken me away and put me in a strait jacket in this warm, black, reeking cell.

Panic welled inside me and I suppressed it, savagely. 'You're all right. Don't cry out. You're thinking clearly. You can remember everything. You were mad, but the attack is over and if you stay quiet and let them see how rational you are, they'll let you go.'

I waited, outwardly calm but with a pounding heart and a whirlpool in my head. Presently I became aware of movement around me. Soft rustlings and sounds of breathing. I listened. There! Faint, regular breathing, and the rustle of sheets. A ward, then. Not a cell. A hospital ward where they tucked you in a bit too tightly. There were others like me, all around. I could have cried with relief. The night-nurse: somewhere, there was bound to be a night-nurse. He, or she, would know something about what had happened to me. More than I knew myself, anyway. I would call. They were used to calls in the night, from patients needing only reassurance. Part of the job.

I called. That is, I tried to call. What actually happened was that I squealed. The sound reverberated, and was answered at once by another squeal. I opened my mouth to say 'Nurse', experimentally; quivering on the edge of panic. The result was a croak. I was voiceless: the victim of some frightful mutilation. The squealing around me continued and there was a sort of flapping, too, as though someone were shaking sheets.

Then something wafted close to my face. Instinctively I threw up an arm to protect myself, and instantly the sensation returned of stiff fingers, enormously long. The limb's movement threw me off balance in some way. My toes lost their grip on whatever it was they were holding and I felt myself falling. Some instinct snapped into operation. I threw out my arms. It seemed to me that I turned over in mid-fall and then my arms were pressed upward, gently, so that my shoulder-blades met across my back. I was no longer falling. I forced my arms downward against the pressure, without knowing why. My body seemed to lift, as though my hands pushed against something solid, though they did not. I had a sensation of speed; of rushing forward and the air on my face.

I became aware that I was squealing, repeatedly; high, short squeals pouring out of me like a stream of machine-gun bullets; striking some distant object and rebounding into my head. Impressions and sensations followed one another so rapidly that my fear was momentarily swamped. A part of me knew that I was flying. At the same time I was aware that my bout of insanity must be continuing. I was frightened, elated, confused, blind; hungry. And superimposed on all these states was an instinct that kept me functioning; hurtling through a blackness strewn with obstacles, yet avoiding collision. Blind, yet not blind.

The realization came to me gradually. There was no shock; no heart-kicking jolt such as I had suffered earlier. Just a slow dawning of the fact that, whatever I might have been before, now I was a bat. In order to assimilate this knowledge thoroughly, I located a resting-place and hung, like one who lies down to digest a heavy meal.

Throughout the world, folklore abounds with tales of lycanthropy: of witches becoming wolves, of hyena-women and leopard-men. All my life I had regarded such things as impossible and yet, why should they be? One tends always to be sceptical about the supernatural. Yet why do we say 'Supernatural'? There must surely be many things in nature we do not know about. Perhaps some of those phenomena which we call supernatural are really parts of nature. Perhaps some of the countless persons who simply 'disappear' become, by a process we know nothing of, other creatures. After all, it had happened to me.

It had happened to me. I do not know how long I hung there, digesting facts and implications. I know that it was hunger that eventually drove me to action, and brought me up against one implication which had not occurred to me. For some time now the other bats, which I now knew were all around me, had been leaving their resting-places in ones and twos. I knew, without knowing *how* I knew, that they were off to feed, and when, at length, an individual close by opened his wings and curved away, down into the darkness, I followed him.

We left the derelict barn, for that is what it was, through a wind-eye. The night was soft and warm, and the soaring elation I felt during those first moments of effortless flight is with me still. The pattern of silvery fields below me, with hedges in black and elms like gouts of smoke, broiling up. The moon, and the silhouette of my wing upon it. The rush of cool air over taut membrane.

I was not to enjoy such unthinking bliss for long. Flight had sharpened my hunger, and now I became aware that all about me bats were feeding. Wheeling and turning they closed with their prey. As it overhauled its victim, each bat would transmit fierce, exultant calls, so that I was reminded of fighter-pilots in pursuit of bombers. The excitement was infectious; a kind of feeding-frenzy, like that which seizes sharks when there is blood in the water. Something crossed my path and I swerved, open-mouthed; salivating. Beating the air. Transmitting, high and rapid, and the echo-pips in my head, faster and faster. Flutter of slipstream on my face and a soft blur ahead, in erratic flight; myself, duplicating every twist, closing.

Heart racing, I thrashed the air and the thing before me came clear in view. The image flashed from eye to brain and I staggered in the air, dropped a wing and turned aside, swept with nausea. The moth fluttered away into the night.

What can I say of the agony that now began for me? How can I hope to convey with mere words the sick horror that rose in me; that kept me circling numbly through that awful feast and sent me famished to my wretched roost at dawn? To be a bat that once was a man: God knows, that was bad enough. But to have a bat's body, a bat's bodily *needs*, and the mind of a man obsessed by his loathing of moths: this surely was the quintessence of Hell?

Now, as I hung pining, a hundred speculations crowded in. How long do bats live? How old a bat was I? How long would this drag on if I refrained from eating; if I starved myself to death? And what choice had I, who became ill at the very *sight* of a moth?

I do not know for how long I hung there. I know that day became night again, at least once. I was aware, dimly, of my companions departing and returning. I know that I mourned for my family and friends, now lost to me for ever. I know also that I prayed for death, and meant it. And the hunger won, at last, as hunger will; overcoming even my life-long revulsion, so that finally, in the worst night of my life, I went forth and ate.

I do not intend to dwell on that night. Suffice it to say that I ate from desperation; impelled by whatever it is that urges a man to self-preservation at any cost; and kept down a little of my loathsome meal, eventually.

Time passed, and little by little I slipped into the rhythm of my new existence: sleeping by day when my thoughts would let me, and flying out at night to hunt. The thrill of the chase remained with me, intensifying if anything, and even the business of eating became faintly pleasurable. And gradually too, my mind grew quiet, until I was sleeping deeply through the shortening days. It became colder. The bats, fat with the summer's gorging, waxed sluggish. Now when we hunted, the night air was thin and there were few moths. We flapped heavily under the bright stars, half-hearted in our pursuits; thinking always of the warm roost.

Until there came a night when we did not go forth at all. I half-woke at the usual hour, moving my eyes only; my limbs warm and numb; cocooned in sleep. Some of those about me awoke too, but none left the roost. They hung drowsing; listening to the sleet-grey, gusty wind. It was hibernation time. One by one, they drifted away into dream-warmth, and left the world to winter.

I too slept, but my sleep was brief and when I awoke I was a man again, in a bed, in a room somewhere. The room was not my room, and the house was not my parents' house. This did not surprise me. I lay, looking at some sad green curtains, knowing I was in another town. Many people had stayed in this room; none for very long. There was a chest of drawers, an alcove with a curtain that did as a wardrobe; a green faded carpet. The dark brown door had a loose knob and down two flights of stairs lived the woman whose house it was.

That's all, really. I worked on a building-site. After a while the job was done and I moved on to the next. And that's what I do. I've been in many towns. I can't remember how many. I take whatever work I can get. I've got my parents' address somewhere, and I keep meaning to write.

People find me strange, so I don't make friends. I hear them sometimes, talking about me when they think I'm not there. 'Leaves his light on all night,' they say. 'And the window open.' Or: 'Where does he go at dinner-time? I've never seen him eat owt.'

Well: they haven't, and they wouldn't like it if they did. It would spoil their appetites, I fancy; all that grey powder round my mouth and those damp, discarded wings beside my plate.

ROBERT SWINDELLS

The Birthday Present

'Mashed, that's what,' old Fatty Scrimshaw said. 'Mashed to a pulp. I tell you there was hardly a brick left standing.'

Old Fatty lives on the same landing as us in the Tower Block and he's always popping in for a chat. Which means gabbing on for hours and hours about the war. Now I don't mind hearing about how the Jerry bombers came zooming over . . . eeeooow eeeooow like that – dropping their load of incendiaries on the middle of our town, and about how you could see the flames as far away as Leicester. Or even about Mrs Fatty running out in her dinky curlers and second best nightie, losing a slipper on the way and yowling louder than a dog when its tail gets trodden on – but not when I've heard it forty-five million times before! It's enough to make your ears drop off.

He was on about it now. Jabbing with his finger at the Marley tiles on our floor.

'Right here where I'm standing. Thirty-eight years to the day it was. A whole row of houses. You know – the kind with the weaver's top-shops. Real nice places and built to last. That's a laugh if you like! Gone in less time than it takes to tell you now, Mrs Hollins.' He wheezed out this gusty sigh and nodded at our Mam.

Mostly when he does that I like to watch because his three chins wobble and he screws up his eyes as the wobble runs up his cheeks, just as if they're made of jelly. He scratches his bald head too, and leaves red marks like railway tracks. But today I wasn't interested. All I wanted was to get out.

'Go on!' Mam roared, because he's deaf as six wads of chewing-gum. Sometimes I think she's quite loony, the things she lets herself in for. But she just says he's lonely, and a bit of time is worth more than a ten-pound note.

'True as the sun rises,' old Fatty said, warming to it. 'On this very

15

spot was where O'Malley lived with his missus and a raft of kids. They were a lively lot, I'll tell you! My stars . . . the things them lads used to get up to. Tricks? Like a cartload of monkeys they were!' He paused and chuckled – remembering. Then he went on: 'Oh yes . . . and over there, more or less under your Kevin's bedroom, was the Dreefes. Mister and his missus and . . .'

I stopped listening and tried to figure out just how I was going to get away from our flat. He was standing right in front of the door, practically sitting on the handle. I measured the space by eye, but it was hopeless. As he's as big as a tractor there was *no way*! If I was to say 'Excuse me', I'd have to yell and then our Mam would want to know where I thought I was going at that time of a Saturday night when our team had been playing Spurs . . . and didn't I ever take a blind bit of notice what she said? You see she's okay about most things, but nutty as nine fruitcakes when it comes to soccer matches and Hooligans – her name for anyone who goes to watch. I've tried telling her she's got it all wrong, but you might as well try pushing a bus over. Not that I'm bonkers about soccer like our Dave. I don't want to see Spurs give us a roasting! But I do *hate* being stuck five floors up on a Saturday, with nothing on telly except some crummy film, and my skateboard screaming at me to come and whizz about on it. And that's another thing our Mam doesn't approve of – skateboards. 'Old Lady Killers' she calls them. She didn't half shred our Dave when he gave me one for my birthday.

'A birthday on the thirteenth and you give him a *skateboard*!' She said in a voice that could've skewered a centipede at long range.

At the time I bristled. Couldn't she see how beautiful it was? All green and silver and strong as a Jumbo Jet. It wouldn't snap at the first bit of stress. I wanted to explain that it was perfectly safe, but knew it was useless. When our Mam gets started, the only thing to do is let her talk till she's tired. So I did.

After, I went for my first fantastic skate. I didn't fall off either. Our Mam looked as if she'd expected me to come home a mangled wreck. But she didn't say so. The talking was over – for the moment!

Now I looked desperately at old Fatty. He'd just got to the bit about coming out of the air-raid shelter next morning and finding Mrs F's unmentionables (his word for her knickers) drooping over a gas-lamp.

'Fancy that, Kevin,' he said, clamping his hand on my shoulder.

I groaned inside. Blazing saddles . . . I hadn't a hope! And then our Mam of all people, came to the rescue.

'Come into the kitchen, Mr Scrimshaw,' she bellowed. 'Sit down and rest your legs. I'll make us a nice cuppa.'

I didn't waste any more time. Reckoning that the tea-making would take about five minutes, I pulled my skateboard from behind our Dave's old cardboard box, where he keeps his motorbike spares, buzzed out of the flat and was three flights down before I heard Mam calling:

'Kev . . . Kevin!'

I kept going. It would mean a belting when I got back, but it was worth it. There were two routes to the place where I was heading. The long way is all streets, but there's a short cut through the cemetery. It's a bit weird when it gets dark. Orange light from the naphtha lamps on the main road, drips through the trees and makes these spidery shapes which grab at you when the wind gets up. There was a stiff breeze now, but I risked it. After all I'd had to hang about long enough already. By this time it was getting pretty dark and the gravestones stood up like giants' mossy teeth – huge and gappy. The breeze made the trees dip and scratch with knotted twig fingers. They aren't too well looked after – the trees I mean – and they hang down low. So you can imagine what I felt like when one combed my hair for me! I did this Olympic jump about six miles high. There was a smell too. I tried to think what it reminded me of, but was in too much of a tearing rush to work it out. I was glad to get shot of the place and reach the jetty, I can tell you! Gave me the creeps it did.

Galloping across the waste ground at the end of the jetty, I arrived at the main road which circles our town. Part of this road is up on stilts with other roads crossing beneath. There's a subway tunnel as well, for people on foot. It forks at the far end – left to the station and right to Jakes Road. Skateboarding isn't allowed, but lots of kids do. It's okay so long as you keep your eyes peeled for nosy parkers who'll tell on you.

It was really dark when I got there. A queer purplish sort of gloom that reached towards the subway, but got cut off by the bright strip lighting. I could hear traffic zooming along the main road. The usual weekend stream of cars making for the pubs. One or two people in their Saturday gear were walking through the subway – no one that mattered. I put my skateboard down. A couple of left-foot pushes and I was on my way, doing this knockout slalom loop round a bloke in cowboy boots and a black velvet suit. Then curving sharp left so as to miss an Indian woman pushing a pram.

There are moments when you feel as if everything has dropped together. Balance, timing, confidence . . . the lot. This was one of those times. All the creepy quakes I'd experienced coming through the cemetery, vanished. I felt terrific. I *was* terrific, as I stood, squatted, leaned and snaked from side to side. Fantastic! But I knew it was going to be seventy million times better coming back. Picking up my skateboard, I started up the slope.

That's when I first saw him. Up at the top he was. A skinny bit of a kid, standing on skates that were much too big. They were a tatty old-fashioned roller pair with steel wheels, and looked really weird on the end of his matchstick legs. I couldn't help wondering where he'd found them – at a jumble sale by the look. His eyes were out on stalks in this pinched-up face as he watched me. He didn't look a little kid somehow. His face had a queer sort of old-young look that made it difficult to guess what age he was. But he wore short trousers – which seemed odd on such a cold November night. Huge hands he had too. Hanging off spindly wrists that were sticking out of a sweater ten miles too short. I must admit I felt a bit narked. He'd better not get in the way, I thought, putting my board down again. I was planning this spectacular nose-wheelie sequence and didn't fancy tangling with a shrimp on rollers out of the ark.

Slap slap with my right foot and I was whooshing along. Both feet on now. Doing a ton across the mouth of the tunnel. Timing perfect as I balanced first on four wheels then on two. I was Boy Skateboard Wonder. Olympic Gold Medal variety!

But I wasn't alone. That kid was just behind. For a minute I felt mad. The nit . . . what did he think he was doing? But I couldn't stay furious. If I was terrific, he was out of this world! There was nothing he couldn't do on those mouldy old skates – turns, spins, figures of eight. I tell you I felt quite jealous!

We swooped up towards the station. I grinned in admiration. I just couldn't help it. And he grinned back. Then, without having to say a word, we set off like one man, as if we'd been practising for weeks. Weaving, turning, cutting across each other with split second precision. It was fabulous! Up at the Jakes Road end I stopped to get my breath. He was just behind and I could see him watching me. There was a kind of hungry look in his eyes and I knew exactly what he wanted.

'Like a go?' I asked – casually, so he wouldn't guess I was itching to try his skates.

He nodded and his pinched white face seemed almost to glow.

'Down and back twice then. Give us your skates.'

We did the swop and I started to buckle on the old skates. I was hearing these queer echoing crashing sounds at the same time, like voices and thunder crackling inside seventy-six empty oil drums. I tried shaking my head and the noise dulled down, but didn't go away. It was a bit rattling. To cover up, I fiddled with the skate straps some more, asking him what he was called.

'Stan.'

The name was in my ears. I wasn't looking straight at him (I was still hunched over my feet) but I could've sworn his mouth didn't move. He stroked my skateboard as if it was a favourite pet cat, then put it down and shoved off just as though he'd been doing it all his life.

'Hang on!' I shouted, standing up and staggering like a drunk as I aimed for the subway entrance where he'd been heading. 'Wait for me!' I felt a right nana, I can tell you. Twice I nearly hit the deck. On my feet his almost magical skates turned into awkward lumbering booby-traps. I lurched forward a few paces. Tipped dangerously. Righted myself – only to find he wasn't there. The noises which had sunk into the background came back, though. Real noises this time. A bunch of yobs in scarves and bobble hats, with football favours pinned to their anoraks, were surging towards me. Most were waving cans of beer. Not their first by the yodels and ear-splitting catcalls that echoed through the subway.

Too late I thought of all Mam's blood-curdling Hooligan tales, as they spotted me and started calling out:

'Here, look what we've found . . .'

'It's Popeye . . .'

'No it ain't . . .'

'Yer it is . . . before he ate his spinach!'

'Give us a go on yer skates, kid . . .'

I wanted to run, but there was no chance with my feet going in all directions. If I'd had my board I might have escaped. In a daft sort of way I half turned, looking for some bolt-hole, and saw Stan at the mouth of the subway. He was on my board – my beautiful skateboard.

The yobs saw too. 'Gerroff that skateboard, Skinny!'

'Beat it, Stan,' I yelled. 'Scram . . . *quick!'*

The next thing I knew was that one of the yobs had hurled a can at me which caught my shin and made me hop and curse. Then, of course, I lost my balance and fell against one of his mates, who shoved me into one of the others, who shoved me back . . . It got a bit rougher each time. They were laughing, but I felt pretty scared. The hairs on the back of my neck prickled, and a strong yearning to be in front of our telly watching that crummy film, hit me. Anywhere would be better than here! I don't know how long they might have gone on tackling and passing me like a human football, but midway from one to another I caught sight of something hurtling towards us. Straight and swift as a bullet it came.

Stan. On my skateboard!

The yobs had seen him as well. They panicked and tried to get out of the way, but everything was happening too fast and there was nowhere to go. I couldn't move. It was just as if the old skates had grown roots and were keeping me plonk in the middle of the subway. In spite of all the racket and jostle, I felt as alone as if I'd been standing on the moon. I was picturing the chaos to come. There'd be a heap of sprawling bodies, and underneath . . . shattered wreckage of plastic, wood and steel.

But it didn't happen like that.

One of the yobs lunged out, meaning to grab Stan and pull him off the board, but froze where he stood and the look on his face could've curdled ten gallons of milk!

For Stan travelled through the lot of us. Yes, *through!* Like a power-boat slicing water. Even now I don't know how it happened. All I remember of the actual moment is a terrible icy cold, deafening silence that cut off the world, and this strong nostril-tingling smell of mildewed biscuits. How long it lasted is another mystery. A second? A year? It seemed like both. Then noises came back. Noises made by running feet as the yobs scattered, scared to death, leaving me stunned and really alone.

No. That's not true. I wasn't quite alone. My skateboard was lodged against the wall at the far end of the tunnel. No Stan. No skates either I realized as I began to run towards it.

Scooping up the skateboard I went on running, my feet taking me

across the waste ground and through the cemetery. Running . . . running . . . not noticing eerie naphtha light or bony tree fingers or mossy gravestone teeth this time. I had one goal – HOME!

When I got there, old Fatty Scrimshaw was still in the kitchen. He hadn't got off his favourite subject.

'Wiped out,' he was saying. 'Every man jack, would you believe?' He shook his bald head.

Our Mam was nodding, eyes glued to his face as if this was the very first time she'd ever heard the story. Quivery though I still was, I couldn't help marvelling at the way she could act. She deserved an Oscar!

Old Fatty brought out a large checked hanky and blew his nose. 'Every man jack . . . except the youngest Dreefe lad. They never did find him. Mind you, a lot went missing that night. Funny lad he was. Quiet. Thin as a piece of string, with great big hands.'

A queer feeling started under my ears and worked down my neck. Like seventy-eight spiders doing a war dance. There was something I wanted to ask, but the question stuck to my teeth.

'Where'd he gone?' our Mam shouted.

A sigh escaped old Fatty and he shrugged his mountain shoulders. 'Out on them old skates his brother give him of course. You couldn't keep him off 'em. Mind you, nobody saw him go. But I reckon that's what happened. He was really taken with them roller skates. Could've gone on the Halls he was that good.' He leaned towards Mam, and under the kitchen light his eyes showed up damp. 'Time and again he used to go to the top of our street, come whizzing down, turn a figure of eight and stop dead at the front door, neat as you please. I tell you, Mrs Hollins, if I had one of them new-fangled fifty pences for every time I've seen him do that, I'd be a rich man now.'

Our Mam seemed wrapped in the story. She hadn't spotted me. 'He can't just've vanished.'

Old Fatty sighed again. 'There were a lot o' bombs fell that night.'

'You mean they didn't find so much as a hair of his head?'

'Not one. Not even a wheel off his skates.'

All this time I'd been standing still as a goal-post, but he looked away from our Mam and straight at me. Little sparks of light flicked off the damp in his eyes, but he wheezed out a laugh and the wobble ran from his chins into the crinkling skin. 'You don't get skates for your birthday and not use 'em, eh, Kevin?'

Our Mam swivelled round in her chair. She was frowning and I started to quake all over again. I heard her say:

'Skating . . .' in her centipede-skewering voice. Then she paused and gave a little snort, staring at me. I saw her grim face relax, and her voice came out sort of croaky: 'You've skated on some pretty thin ice tonight, me lad!' Picking up the biscuit tin, she held it out. She was *almost* smiling.

I took a Jammy Dodger and bit it. The smell was oat-sweet, gooey, biscuity. Then I remembered, and there wasn't any need for my question. That was it – biscuits . . . *mouldy* biscuits. The graveyard smell. I *knew*. The whole story nearly spilled out of me then and there, specially with old Fatty still damp around the eyes. Maybe it would help if I told? But something held me back.

Our Mam got up to put the kettle on again and I slipped into my bedroom, shutting the door.

'That's two I owe you, Stan,' I said, quiet like so no one else would hear. 'Thanks!'

After all, how am I to know when I might need saving again?

MARJORIE DARKE

Just a Guess

The first thing you noticed about Joe was the colour of his eyes. The table where Philip sat was close to Miss Atkinson's desk, and that morning she brought Joe into the classroom with her and stood him by her while she sat down and got out her register. All the children, boys and girls alike, were staring at the newcomer, some directly, some in a sideways fashion. There were some grins, a giggle or two. Joe looked around the room, and his eyes, Philip noticed, were a brilliant green. Cat's eyes. The bell rang.

'Good morning, children,' said Miss Atkinson.

'Good morning, Miss Atkinson. Good morning all.'

'Answer your names, please.'

Reading the register took long enough for everyone to have a good look at Joe. He was tallish, thinnish, and his clothes were not very smart. His face was very brown, his hair dark, long, a bit greasy. He did not seem embarrassed.

'Now children,' said Miss Atkinson, 'as you can see, Top Class has grown by one this morning. This is Joe Sharp. His family has just come to stay . . . that is, to live . . . in the village. Quite a large family too, I believe. You're the youngest, aren't you, Joe?'

'Yes, miss.'

'And how many brothers and sisters have you?'

'No sisters, miss. Just six brothers.'

'A seventh son, are you?' said Miss Atkinson, looking up.

I wonder, she thought, is it possible, could he be the seventh son of a . . .

'Yes, miss,' said Joe. 'My father is too.'

'Oh,' said Miss Atkinson. 'Yes. Well, now then, let me see.'

She looked round the class. 'Philip. Philip Edwards. You're a sensible person. I want you to look after Joe if you will please.

Everything will be strange for him at first. Show him where everything lives. All right?'

'Yes, Miss Atkinson,' Philip said. He saw the green eyes looking at him, and suddenly, for an instant, they shut, both together, in a kind of double wink.

'Now, Joe,' said Miss Atkinson. 'You sit next to Philip, there's room for you there, and I'll get you some exercise books. The rest of you, look at the blackboard please, and get on with the work I've put up there. Later on this morning we have an interesting visitor coming in to school to talk to you – I'll tell you . . . no, I don't think I will. We'll leave it as a surprise.'

She got up and went to the big stock cupboard at the far side of the room.

'Interesting visitor!' whispered Philip across the table.

'Hope it's Kenny Dalglish!'

'Kevin Keegan,' whispered a boy opposite. 'Kenny Dalglish is rubbish!'

'Football!' sneered a girl, wrinkling her nose.

'Copper,' said Joe very quietly.

'What?'

'It'll be a copper.'

'How do *you* know?'

'Just a guess.'

'Shhh.'

Miss Atkinson came back with a handful of books, a pencil, a ruler, a rubber.

When the bell went for morning playtime Philip said to the new boy 'Come on then. You'd better come with me. Better put your coat on, it's cold.'

'I haven't got one,' said Joe.

'Oh,' said Philip. He put on his new anorak, blue with a red stripe down each arm and a furry hood. He felt a little awkward. 'Birthday present,' he said.

'November the twenty-third,' said Joe.

'What?' said Philip in amazement.

'Just a guess.'

'How . . . oh, I get it,' said Philip. 'You looked at the register. While Miss Atkinson was talking. You must have sharp eyes.'

'Yes,' said Joe.

In the roaring, screaming, galloping playground the two boys stood in a sheltered corner. Philip didn't feel he could dash off to play Bulldog with his particular friends, and the December winds were cold for someone without a top coat, specially somebody as thin as this one. He took a Penguin out of his anorak pocket.

'Have a bit?' he said.

'No thanks,' said Joe. 'Don't want to spoil my appetite for lunch. It's my favourite.'

'What is?'

'Spam fritters and chips.'

Clever Dick, thought Philip, I've got him this time. He hasn't seen the list in the hall. He's just a know-all. It's roast beef.

'Want to bet?,' he said.

'I haven't any money,' Joe said.

'Well, I'll tell you what,' Philip said. He put his hand in his trouser pocket. 'I've got this 10p piece, see? If it is Spam fritters and chips for lunch, I'll give it to you, just give it to you. If you're wrong, well, you needn't give me anything.' That's fair, he thought. After all I do actually *know* it's roast beef.

'All right,' said Joe. The green eyes looked straight into Philip's and then shut suddenly, momentarily, in that curious double wink. Philip wanted to smile back, but he felt embarrassed and began to flip the 10p piece in the air, using the pressure of thumb against forefinger, the proper way, the way referees did. He had only lately learned to do this and was proud of it.

Joe stood by him silently, shivering a little in the cold wind. A gang of younger boys dashed past, and one shouted 'Who's your friend then, Phil?' A group of small girls in woolly hats cantered by, driving each other in harnesses made of skipping ropes. The horses neighed and the drivers cried 'Gee up!' and 'Steady!'

'Heads,' said Joe suddenly. Philip, who had been catching the coin on the back of his left hand and covering it with the fingers of his right, exposed the result of the latest toss. It was a head.

'Try again,' Philip said. He tossed the coin three times and each time Joe called correctly.

'You couldn't get it right ten times running,' said Philip, 'I bet you couldn't. Want to bet?'

'I haven't got any money,' Joe said.

'Oh, it doesn't matter. Just try it.'

Philip tossed his 10p piece ten times. Each time Joe called correctly. Philip scratched his head.

'How d'you do that?' he said.

'Just a guess.'

'You're just lucky, I reckon. Let's try it again.'

'No time,' Joe said. 'It's twenty to eleven. The bell will go any second.'

Philip looked at Joe's thin bare wrists.

'How do you know?' he said. 'You haven't got a watch.'

The bell rang.

As they joined the rush back into school, Philip remembered what Miss Atkinson had said about an interesting visitor. What had Joe said? 'Copper.' I shouldn't be surprised, Philip found himself thinking, and then a funny shiver ran down his spine as they entered the classroom. The curtains were drawn, a screen was set up against one wall, and cables snaked across the floor to a film projector on Miss Atkinson's desk. She stood behind it, and beside her was the uniformed figure of a tall police sergeant.

'Sit down quietly, children,' said Miss Atkinson. Philip forced himself not to look at his neighbour. He didn't want to see that double wink. His mind felt swimmy. Dimly he heard snatches of talk ... 'Sergeant Harrison ... Road Safety Division.... film to show you ...', and then a deep voice asking questions ... 'How ... When ... What would you do ...?'

Hands were shooting up everywhere, and once he was conscious of Joe's voice answering something.

'Good. Very good indeed,' said the sergeant. 'I didn't expect anyone to know that one. How did you know, son?'

'Just a guess.'

Then the projector began to run. It was a good film, an interesting film designed to catch and hold children's attention, and gradually Philip began to concentrate on it. It ended with a simulated road accident, where a boy dashed suddenly across a road, right under the wheels of a double-decker bus. It was very realistic.

The projector fell silent, and the only noise in the classroom was a thin metallic ssswish as Miss Atkinson opened the curtains. The sun had come out, and the audience blinked at the sudden light.

'One last thing,' said Sergeant Harrison in his deep voice.

'One last piece of advice I've got for you lot. You've proved to me this morning that you know quite a bit about the Green Cross Code. You've answered most of my questions pretty well.' He looked at

Joe. 'One of them very well. I shouldn't have expected any local lad to have been able to answer that particular one.'

'Joe's new, Sergeant,' said Miss Atkinson. 'It's his first day. His people are travellers – you may have seen their caravans on the common. I expect he's been all over the place, have you, Joe?'

'Yes, miss.'

'Ah, gypsy are you?' said Sergeant Harrison, but he did not say it unkindly, and he smiled as he said it.

'Yes, sir.'

'Reckon you'll be here long?'

'No, sir.'

Philip felt a sudden ache.

'Anyway,' said the sergeant. 'As I was saying. Here's one last piece of advice. You all saw how that film finished. Well, don't . . . think . . . it . . . can't . . . happen . . . to . . . you. We all know that was only a mock-up. The boy acting the part didn't get killed, of course. But boys do, and girls, somewhere, every day of every week of every year. So don't think "that couldn't be me". It could. So take care.'

'Paint monitors,' said Miss Atkinson a quarter of an hour later, when the screen and projector had been stowed away, and the tall sergeant had put on his peaked cap and gone. 'Angela. Sue. Judith. Would you please put the tables ready after you've had your lunch. That film should have left us all with lots of pictures in our minds. This afternoon we'll see if we can put them on paper. Now go and wash your hands, everybody, and line up by the hall door.'

Standing beside Joe in the queue, Philip listened to the pair in front.

'What is it today?'

'Roast beef.'

'Ugh!'

'Don't you like it?'

'Not much.'

They all trooped in, and when places had been settled and grace said, Mrs Wood the cook appeared in the doorway of the kitchen.

'I'm sorry, children,' she said, 'there's been a bit of a mix-up. The beef for today's lunch didn't turn up, but I don't think you'll be too disappointed.' She paused.

Philip put his hand in his pocket.

'It's Spam fritters and chips,' she said.

There were one or two 'Oh's', a loud murmur of 'MMM!s'.

'Quiet, please,' said the teacher on dinner duty.

'Keep it,' whispered Joe. 'You keep it.' Philip took his hand out of his pocket. He looked at Joe and got the double wink.

After lunch, in the playground, everybody knew. Top Class had told the rest, and somehow everyone except the littlest ones managed to pass close to the spot where Philip and Joe were standing. A gypsy! There was giggling. Philip could hear some of the passing comments and they were not kind. 'My dad says they're dirty.' 'They nick things.' 'Horses.' 'Babies.' More giggles. 'They eat hedgehogs.' A snort of laughter.

'Can you tell fortunes, diddakoi?' said Mickey Bean, a big boy who was always looking for trouble and finding it. He stood in front of Joe, quite close, picking his nose with his thumb. Philip felt himself grow suddenly, furiously, angry.

'I can, Mickey,' he said in a choky voice, 'and yours is, you'll get your face smashed in.'

Mickey Bean took his thumb out and clenched his fist.

'Why, you ...' he began, but Joe said quietly 'Pack it in.' He looked at Mickey with his green eyes, and after a moment Mickey looked away.

'Come on, Phil,' said Joe, and they walked off together.

'That was nice of you,' he said, 'sticking up for me.'

They stood side by side at the far end of the playground, their fingers hooked through the wire mesh of the boundary fence, and stared at the traffic going up and down the village street. Philip swallowed.

'Can you?' he said. 'Tell fortunes, I mean?'

'Fortunes?' Joe said. 'I dunno about fortunes. I know what's going to happen. Sometimes. Not always of course.'

'Well, could you ...' Philip looked around, '... could you ... tell what will be the next thing to come round the corner, down there, at the end of the street?'

'Probably,' Joe said. 'Want to bet?' he said, and he gave the double wink, very quickly. The twinkling of an eye, two eyes rather, thought Philip, grinning.

'I haven't got any money,' he said. 'What's in my pocket is yours, really.'

'Well, all right then, if I'm wrong,' said Joe, 'it's yours again.'

'O.K.,' Philip said. They stared down the street, empty for a moment.

'Private car,' Joe said. '"S" Registration. 4-door. Pale blue. Lady driving.' He paused. 'It's a Ford.'

They waited five, ten seconds. Suddenly a car came round the wall of the end house in the street, and drove up towards them, and passed them. It was a 4-door 'S' Registration saloon with a lady at the wheel. It was pale blue.

'It's a Vauxhall,' Philip said slowly. He looked sideways at Joe.

'Just a guess,' Joe said. 'You have a go,' he said.

Philip tried 'Red car' and got a bicycle, 'Lorry' and got the post van, 'Bus' and round the corner came an old Morris 1000. 'It's Miss Atkinson,' he said as it drew near and began to indicate to turn in to the school road. 'I expect she's been down to Beezer's, she often does at lunch-time.' Beezer's was the village shop which sold every-thing you could imagine, and Philip was about to explain this to the new boy when it occurred to him that he needn't bother. Joe prob-ably knew exactly what she'd bought. Before he could voice the thought, Joe said, 'All right, if you really want to know – a small brown loaf, six oranges, and a packet of Daz. Oh, and something wrapped in newspaper. Not sure what it is. It's dirty, I think.'

And of course when Miss Atkinson had disappeared into the school, and they wandered down and peeped in the car, there they were on the back seat, bread, fruit, soap-powder, and a head of celery.

Philip's earlier feeling about Joe, a scary feeling that the green eyes could somehow see into the future, had already altered quite a bit. It wasn't a feeling now, it was a certainty, and therefore not as fright-ening, though just as exciting.

'I suppose you know what I'm going to paint this afternoon,' he said.

'Yes,' Joe said.

At that moment the bell rang for afternoon school. The tables were ready, covered with old newspapers, the paints, brushes, palettes, and mixing dishes put out.

'Painting aprons, everybody, and sleeves rolled tightly, please,' said Miss Atkinson. 'Joe Sharp, I've got an old shirt for you from my odds-and-ends cupboard.'

I know exactly what I'm going to paint, thought Philip. How

curious that someone else does too. Before I've even made a mark on the paper.

He began to draw with a pencil, little figures, lots of them, like matchstick men. It was to be a picture of the children coming out of school and crossing the road. With Mrs Maybury the lollipop lady. And lots of cars and buses and lorries and motorbikes. He was so absorbed that it was some time before he realized that Joe's paper was still quite blank.

'What's the matter, Joe?' said Miss Atkinson, coming round. 'Aren't you feeling well?'

'Too many Spam fritters,' someone said, and there was giggling.

'I'm all right, miss,' Joe said softly.

'Well, come along then. You must make a start. Think about this morning's film. Haven't you got some sort of picture in your mind?'

'Yes, miss,' Joe said. He picked up a brush and began to put paint on his piece of paper, big splashes of it, with big brush strokes, very quickly. Miss Atkinson went away, and Philip began to colour in his matchstick men, carefully, neatly. He forgot about Joe or indeed anybody else in the room until he heard Miss Atkinson's voice again.

'Why, Joe,' she said, 'that's a strange picture. What's it supposed to be?'

'It's an accident, miss,' Joe said, and Philip, turning to look, found the green eyes fixed on him with the strangest expression. Quickly Philip looked at Joe's picture. There were no figures in it, no shapes. There were just splodges of colour on a background of bluey-black. At one side there was something that might have been a tree, or a post perhaps, with a stripy trunk bent over in the middle, an orange blob on the end of it. Under that there was a red squidge, and in the middle of the painting a kind of chequered path with a big dark mass on it.

'Yes,' Miss Atkinson said. 'I see.'

'What is it?' Philip whispered when she had gone away. 'What's the matter? Why are you looking at me like that?'

'It's nothing,' Joe said, and then suddenly, violently, he jumped to his feet, knocking over his chair, and picking up his painting he tore it noisily across, in half, then into quarters, and then again and again till there wasn't a piece bigger than a postage stamp. Everyone stared open-mouthed.

'Joe!' cried Miss Atkinson. 'What in the world . . .? Look, young man, I don't give out good quality paper and expensive paints so that you can . . .' She stopped, seeing the curious pallor in the brown face. 'Are you quite sure you're feeling all right?'

'Yes, miss. Sorry, miss,' Joe said.

'Well, it's too late to start again now,' Miss Atkinson said.

'Put all those scraps into the wastepaper basket. The rest of you, finish off as soon as you can and start tidying up.'

'Wait for me,' Joe said, when they had been dismissed and were crossing the road with a crowd of others under Mrs Maybury's eagle eye. It was raining and misty and getting dark all at once, and the water ran off the lollipop lady's cap and yellow oilskins. There was only one pavement in this part of the street, so everybody crossed before turning their separate ways.

'We can walk down together,' Philip said. 'If your, um, caravan's on the common, I live down that way. Our house is called . . .' 'I know,' said Joe. 'Of course,' Philip said.

'The only difference is,' he went on, 'that you can stay on this side now, but I cross over the zebra.'

'Between Beezer's and the Post Office,' Joe said.

'Yes.'

'You *mustn't*.'

'What?'

'You mustn't. Whatever you do, you mustn't go on that zebra crossing tonight.'

'Oh, but look,' Philip said, 'I promised Mum I'd always use the crossing. The traffic whizzes along here. And you heard what the policeman said this morning about zebras.'

'You mustn't,' Joe said doggedly, the rain running down his hair and making it look longer and greasier than ever.

'It was that painting of yours, wasn't it?' said Philip.

'You sort of saw something in it, did you?' Joe nodded.

'Yes, but after all that's just ...'

'Just a guess,' Joe said.

Philip stopped and looked into the green eyes. They shut, quickly, in the double wink, and Philip grinned.

'Oh, all right,' he said, 'if it makes you any happier I'll cross over earlier.'

They walked on a bit till they came opposite the Post Office, where there was a pavement on each side of the street. Philip looked left, looked right, looked left again, and went carefully over.

They walked on, on opposite sides now, till they came to the zebra crossing, where they stopped and faced one another across the road. It was nearly dark, and the street lights made yellow reflections in the pools of water glistening on the road.

'G'night then, Joe,' Philip called. 'See you in the morning,' but any answer was drowned in a sudden squealing of brakes. The red sports car, travelling fast, tried too suddenly to stop at the sight of two boys, both apparently about to cross. The tyres found no grip on the wet surface and the car skidded wildly sideways, straight at Joe.

Philip heard a crash as it hit the Belisha beacon, which broke, almost in the middle, so that the top part with its orange ball came slowly down like a flag lowered to half mast.

'He guessed wrong! He guessed wrong! He guessed wrong!' went racing through Philip's brain. He had not seen Joe's wild leap to safety. The car obscured it, and the rain, and the gloom.

'Joe! Joe!' Philip shouted, and he ran madly across the zebra crossing.

He did not see the lorry, and the lorry did not see him. Until the last moment.

Which was too late.

DICK KING-SMITH

The Demon Kite

Mahyar lived in a large house surrounded by a spacious garden. Outside his front gate ran the main road and across the road there was a huge field known to all the people of the town as the *maidan*. Mahyar's father was very rich, he was the Director of the Devi Cotton Mills. In their house they had seven servants, counting the chauffeur who was paid by the mill to drive Mahyar's father and his family around in the two cars which they owned.

On Saturdays Mahyar's friends would come to his house, friends he made in the posh school to which he went. On weekdays Mahyar was alone. He'd do his homework and sometimes he'd go to the *maidan* with the young servant who ran errands for the cook and the bearer, whom everyone called Boy.

The most popular game of the hot months was kite fights. The poor boys of the city would gather in the *maidan* in pairs and gangs and fly kites. The sky above the *maidan* would be dotted with the colours of the tissue paper stretched on a cross of bamboo sticks. If you actually stood next to the flyers, you could see the cat's cradle of threads, all tense and coloured, making a skein across the sky. The thread of the kites was not just ordinary thread. It was made by passing number ten thickness cotton through a hot can full of gelatine and crushed glass. The thread was dipped through this sticky, lethal mixture and left out in the sun to dry. When it was dry, it was deadly. If you ran it through your fingers and held your finger tight around it, the greens and blues of the cotton would come away crimson with your blood. The flyers would launch their kites into the sky and bring them down and the thread of one kite would graze against the thread of another and the sharp, glassy length would cut through the thread of the opposing kite.

Mahyar had lost a few kite fights himself. Boy had held the reel of glassed thread as Mahyar manipulated his kite across the sky, reeling and dipping and challenging the others on the *maidan*. He knew the heavy pull of the expensive kite when it got to the upper reaches of the breeze. He knew the sudden lightness, the limp and defeated feeling when his own kite was cut.

The kites which were cut floated away. They were chased by the boys on the *maidan* who brandished branches of trees and long bamboo sticks to entangle the thread of the cut kite and catch it and claim it for themselves.

The champion flyer in all the *maidan* was a boy named Datta. Datta was a poor boy and he didn't have any money to buy kites for himself, but he always had a kite to fly because he made it his business to chase the cut kites and claim them when he caught them.

Mahyar knew the names of all the different varieties of kite that flew in the *maidan*. His friends from school didn't know such things. If they flew kites, they flew them with the help of their fathers or servants from the terraces of their houses, far away from where the poor boys gathered for the great game. Mahyar knew that the kite with two balanced triangles, was called a *bhowra*, a top; the one with a central piece and two triangular fins on either side was called a *machhli*, a fish; and a single coloured one was called a *rangi*, a coloured one.

One evening at the end of the hot season a strange kite appeared in the sky above the *maidan*. Mahyar was sitting in his room doing his homework. He was doing fractions and feeling quite proud that he knew his seventeen times table so well that his teacher had asked him to start writing in an ordinary lined book instead of in the squared ones they used in the lower classes.

Just then Boy rushed up.

'Have you seen the *patang*, Mahyar *baba*,' he said. 'The kite, it's like a second sun in the sky. Nobody knows who's flying it. It's got a straight thread and it's coming from far across the trees in Koregaon Park. Just like an electric wire, strong like that.'

'Wait two minutes for me,' Mahyar said, 'and wait quietly because seven seventeens are 119 plus four which gives 123.' Mahyar put his pen down. He leaned out of the window for a good look.

The kite was very high up now and several others rose from the *maidan* to challenge it. Its colours were very clear. It was red with a pattern of crescent moons in yellow and blue and black near its four corners. It was a diamond shape and not the usual stretched square.

It had two drooping moustaches of silver hanging over the smile of the bottom crescent.

'Let's go,' Mahyar said, and he and Boy ran out of the house and out of the gate and into the *maidan*.

From the *maidan* he thought he could see the light of the sun bouncing off the surface of the kite, like a mirror throwing flashes over the crowd. The thread of the kite was purple and it glistened with what looked like globules of very shiny glass.

'Maybe someone is flying it from a terrace in Bund Garden Road,' Mahyar said.

'Not possible,' Boy said, 'Datta's men have even cycled out to find where it's coming from and they said it goes beyond the hills even, right over the town.'

'Don't be idiotic.'

'Yes, I'm telling you, it goes on and on like a railway line.'

Mahyar saw two other kites ascend from different ends of the field. One large blue and green *bhowra* was clearly intent on a fight. The crowd gave a little shout as the '*page*', the kite-fight, commenced. The *bhowra* was sent gliding slowly out and then brought with a jerk into a dive on to the thread of the alien kite and then released again. It quivered in the wind. For a whole second it hesitated as thread met thread and then floated away on the wind like a hand waving goodbye. The crowd shouted again. The flyer had dropped his reel of thread and was running across the *maidan*, together with fifty other boys, to retrieve the cut kite.

'It has to be soda thread,' Mahyar said.

Then he spotted Datta who stood in a cluster of boys. They weren't going to run for the kite. It was funny. One of the boys from the gang heard Mahyar's remark to Boy about the thread.

'What soda thread,' he said. 'It's got electric thread, every time it cuts a kite, some sparks come out of it.'

'It's a demon kite,' Datta said. 'Demons have to be brought down.'

He was staring at the crescent wonder, standing fixed on the grass of the *maidan* in bare feet, his legs sticking out of the threadbare, rolled-up hems of his cotton trousers.

Mahyar knew that the boys in his gang were waiting for Datta's word.

'I've seen demon kites before. Slowly, day after day it'll rake the stiffness out of the breeze over our *maidan*. We'll never be able to fly

38

kites here again.' Datta was quite firm about what he said. The twilight was fast upon them.

'Why are we standing here. We can catch all the kites that the demon cuts,' one of the boys in the gang said.

'You first-born always talk like idiots,' Datta said. 'Once a kite had been cut by the demon kite, it's good for nothing; it won't take the wind. You watch.'

As he spoke the demon kite began to glide slowly further away from where they stood. It moved steadily, as though it were a cousin of the clouds themselves.

'We'll get some wire tomorrow if it's still here, and tie it to stones and bring the devil down.'

'Where's it going?' Boy asked. He was addressing his question to Datta.

'It's looking for your sister,' one of the other boys said.

'It's going where the sun hasn't yet set,' Datta said.

Over dinner Mahyar told his dad about the demon kite. Only he didn't say it was a demon kite. That sort of talk was not tolerated in the house. His dad said that someone was probably flying it from the water tower, because that was the highest point in the town.

'Some boys were saying it's a demon kite,' Mahyar said.

'Uneducated people. They'll believe anything,' his father said.

The next day in school Mahyar thought about the kite . . . He'd looked for it in the morning, out of the window of the car, but it wasn't above the *maidan*. He didn't say a word about it to his school friends, because they'd laugh at him for believing what the street boys believed.

The kite became a beacon in the evening sky. Everyone now knew that it was a very powerful kite, the strongest they had ever seen, but most believed that it was being flown from the water tower. Some of the regular gangs of the *maidan* began to ignore the demon kite and fight their own battles in the far corner. Mahyar would stay in his room and after finishing his homework he would sit at the window and watch the demon kite from there, dancing, curving, diving like a swallow, seeming to show off now to try and attract attention it had lost by standing still. Mahyar could see that Datta's gang was no longer with him. They darted about the *maidan* with branches and bamboos.

Mahyar thought about the kite a lot. He knew that Datta was thinking about it too. If Datta was right and it was a demon kite, then possessing it would give him power over the whole *maidan*. It would be something like possessing a death-ray pistol, or like having Batman as your personal friend.

Then the rains came. When the rains actually came down hard, Mahyar saw that people were more bothered about keeping themselves dry than about watching the antics of the demon kite.

Mahyar had stopped going to the *maidan*, he was playing records on the portable player that his father had bought him. He glimpsed out of the window beyond the sleepy weepy roots of the banyan tree. The *maidan* was deserted, he could see a lone figure standing in the centre of the field. It was Datta, standing there with his kite-catching branch looking up at the sky. Mahyar looked up automatically, searching the sky for the demon kite, but it was no longer there. Not even a demon flyer would launch a kite into a sky full of black clouds. Datta had gone crazy. Even Boy said he'd gone crazy and that's why his gang had left him.

Then it caught his eye. As he turned away from the record player, Mahyar could see the demon kite low in the centre of the *maidan*. He was surprised. It couldn't have flown on the wind that fast. Why had its flyer launched it? Was there a flyer? There weren't any other kites that evening, only the black clouds, scattered and frowning and threatening to gang together and storm down. Then a thought struck Mahyar. The kite had come to challenge the clouds. Stupid. It seemed closer than it had been before and he could see funny patterns, like writing in a strange language around its crescent moons.

Mahyar noticed that the light was dying and clouds came on thicker from over the trees and yet the demon kite looked brighter than it ever had. It'd better go back from where it had come, he thought. He saw Datta following its progress across the *maidan* and upwards towards the clouds. Then just as the rain began to fall, there was the crash of distant thunder. The drops fell on the leaves of the banyan tree and made a sound like an army marching. Datta still stood in the centre of the field, absolutely still.

The kite was still climbing, reaching up to the clouds. And it shone and the silver writing around the crescents looked like writhing snakes as it glistened. It's not beautiful, Mahyar thought, it's really a demon kite. He couldn't see its thread even though he strained his eyes. It was getting dark fast. Then a flash of lightning shot from the clouds just above the kite. Mahyar was amazed. In the flash he saw

40

the purple thread of the kite, and he thought he saw it being hit by the lightning. He was right. The kite turned like a person falling backwards. It hit the wind horizontally and then like any other kite separated from its flyer, it began to glide on the layers of air.

As he looked out of the window, Mahyar was sure that no one but he and Datta had seen the demon kite's fight with the lightning. Datta was beginning to run. Mahyar felt his heart pounding. He dashed out of his room, down the stairs and into the garden. In a moment he was across the street and on the *maidan*. Maybe I should get a bamboo out of the garage, he thought, Datta has a branch. But his feet were faster than his thoughts. I've got to catch it, I've got to fight to catch it, he was thinking.

He looked up and saw that the kite was coming to him. So was Datta. The kite flew low now. It was bigger than he'd thought. It had a huge grin on its face. It was steadily coming down. Mahyar sighted its thread that trailed behind, a long loop disappearing into the grass thirty yards from him.

Mahyar stopped running. All Mahyar had to do was wait till the thread glided over him and grab it. He'd won the race.

He waited and then leapt for the thread, losing sight of the kite which was at the edge of the *maidan* near the road. All he could see now was the glitter of the thread and he felt it rasping through his closed fist. Mahyar grabbed it and began hauling it in across the grass, trying to pull in as much of the loose trail before Datta got to it. He wrapped it frantically round his left arm and he turned to see where the kite had glided. Just as he felt the weight of the kite on the thread he was aware of the panting breath of Datta on him.

'Leave that thread go, slippery little brat,' Datta said.

'I caught it first,' Mahyar said. 'It's mine, I've got it. I caught this kite.'

'You give me that thread,' Datta said.

'No, it's mine,' Mahyar said as he ran after the kite which was slowly, majestically crossing the road. Datta grabbed for the thread. Suddenly Mahyar realized that to Datta it wasn't a game. Winning and losing were part of a game but the catching of the demon kite was not a game. As they crossed the street together, jostling and digging each other in the ribs, they could see the demon kite hesitating on the air. Then it sliced itself in one smooth sweep into Mahyar's garden and the waiting branches of the banyan tree. There it hung, horizontal and lethargic. The thread in Mahyar's hand went limp. Datta's hand grabbed Mahyar's wrist and the purple thread wrapped around it. In a deft movement, Datta caught the thread beyond Mahyar's arm and snapped it.

'It's my kite, it's in my tree, I caught it fair and square,' Mahyar said.

Datta wasn't paying any attention. He had run up to the garden wall and was trying to jerk the kite out of its perch in the tree.

'That's my house,' Mahyar said.

Datta was looking round with the practised look of a boy who scaled walls and ran the risks that private gardens offered.

Mahyar ran towards the gate. At least he'd be the first up the tree. As he reached it he could see that Datta had climbed on top of the wall and was jerking at the thread frantically. Mahyar could hear the paper of the kite thrashing about against the leaves of the banyan tree.

'I'll call my servants,' Mahyar said.

He heard Datta laugh. Datta was jerking harder now and though neither of them could see where the kite had disappeared in the thick foliage of the banyan tree, they could hear it. It was like birds having a fight.

'Don't you have any respect for the demon kite?'

'What demon kite, it's just an ordinary kite. If you're going to call your servants, I'll tear it up from here before I run.'

'Suppose I give you some money?'

'For what?'

'For leaving it alone.'

'How much?'

'Four rupees.'

'Where's the money?'

'If you give me the thread I'll get it.'

'All right, four rupees for the thread.'

Mahyar turned, ran upstairs to his room and pulled the notes out of the leather wallet in his chest of drawers. He counted four rupees as he ran out again. He held the notes up to Datta who took them, tucked them in his trousers and jumped off the wall on to the road. Without a word of thanks to Mahyar, he crossed the road, picked up his kite-catching branch and disappeared on to the dark of the *maidan*. Mahyar watched him go.

The kite was his now. He'd take it down in the morning. It was the first kite he'd ever caught. He wouldn't tell Boy about the kite, he'd

42

just get up early and climb and get it and paper over any cracks and tears it may have suffered. Then in the evening he'd take it to the terrace and fly it. He wouldn't risk going to the *maidan*. The boys on the *maidan* would all look up and see him flying the demon kite and they wouldn't know how it had fallen from its pedestal in the sky into his hands.

He slept lightly that night and woke up to what he thought were footsteps on the gravel outside. The window, which he'd left open, was lit by the moon. Mahyar lay under the quilt and listened. There was some sound outside. He got out of bed and went to the window. A sight awaited him. The demon kite had loosened itself from the upper branches and hung a few yards from his window. The kite shone in the moonlight and cast a glow around itself. Mahyar scratched himself on the thigh through his pyjamas to make sure he was awake.

The red of the demon kite looked like the colour of ripe water melon. The crescents grinned. The colours in the crescents began to look to Mahyar like the teeth of a smile; the patterns around them, silver and grey, like a haze cast around the paper. As he stared at it, it looked to him like the sail of a pirate ship with a skull spread over it; then it looked red and blue and shone with golden streaks like the fan of a peacock, and still he looked at it and he thought it changed as he looked, into the tawny face of an owl. The demon kite fluttered and its motion was like the sweep of a curtain hanging in the doorway of some palace in a desert; and then it looked to him like the standard borne in the air by the bearers of a barbarian chief leading an army on horseback; a mask worn by a dancer; the face of a wise man from China; a basket of striped snakes; a rider plunging over the moon; a drowned galleon; the sad eyes of a prince who has lost an empire; the pattern of a cobweb; a car on a mountain railway in a stormy night; a hanged man.

The kite dangled just three yards away from his reach in the leaves of the banyan tree. Mahyar realized that the thud and crunch he'd heard were real footsteps. He looked away from the kite as he heard the rustling of the branches and he saw the silhouette of a boy climbing the forks and knuckles of the tree towards where the kite hung. He wanted to cry out but he didn't because the night was too silent for his voice to disturb. He knew it was Datta.

As Datta reached the coil of thread which held the kite to the tree, Mahyar saw the sharp sheen of a switchknife blade.

43

'I thought I bought that kite from you.' His voice came out in a pleading whisper.

'You think you can buy anything? Call the police if you like,' Datta said cutting the demon kite loose from its harness. Datta began to climb down the tree again.

'Datta,' Mahyar said.

'So you know my name, then slippery.'

'You know I caught it first. I got the thread before you.'

'I'm not playing that game any more,' Datta said.

'I'll give you five more rupees.'

'What? Five rupees for a demon kite?'

'You said it wasn't a demon kite.'

Datta was now at the bottom of the tree picking up the kite and winding the loose thread in a figure of eight on his outstretched thumb and little finger. Mahyar knew there was nothing he could do to stop him. Even so, the words came out of his mouth.

44

'How much do you want for it?'

'You can't fly this kite from your terrace. It doesn't belong in your garden or to you. Ask your father to buy you one from the bazaar. Only a demon flyer can make this a demon kite again.' Datta said, hauling the kite over his shoulder like a great cape and Mahyar caught the glint of the moon shining from his eyes as he turned and made for the gate.

FARRUKH DHONDY

The Boy's Story

'Tell me a story. A ghost story,' the boy said.

'I don't know any stories about ghosts,' the father answered.

'Haven't you ever seen a ghost?' the boy asked.

'No.'

'Hasn't anyone you've ever known seen a ghost?'

'No.'

'How do you know? Someone might have seen a ghost and you didn't know about it.'

'People I know don't see ghosts. They're not that sort,' the father said.

'What sort of people see ghosts?' the boy pursued.

'I don't know. Weird people. Not anyone like you and me.'

The boy sighed. Ordinary people, it seemed, like his father and himself, didn't see ghosts. Where, then, were the ghosts? Who saw them? Who wrote ghost stories? Only the weirdos? Where did they get their ideas from? He tried again.

'If you saw a ghost now, what would you do?'

'Here? In the middle of the town? In daylight?'

'It's not all that daylight now. But suppose you were all alone here in the middle of the night, and you saw a ghost. What would you do then?'

'How would I know it was a ghost?' the father asked. He was a practical man. Or so he always said.

'You'd know,' the boy said, confident.

'I should take no notice,' the father said.

'Suppose it started coming after you?'

'If I wasn't taking any notice of it, I wouldn't know it was coming after me, would I?'

'You'd feel it coming. Not running. Slowly.'

'Exactly where do I see this ghost?' the father asked, humouring his son.

The boy thought. He looked around the crowded street. He looked at the bright shop windows, sprinkled with imitation frost and dressed in sparkling silver and gold and in scarlet, for Christmas. He looked at the massed cars, moving snail-pace along the crowded street, at the tall double-decker buses full of faces peering out through the steamed-up windows. He tried to imagine the place dark, silent and deserted. It was difficult, now that it was all cheerful bustle and glitter, the pavements thronged with other shoppers, carrying gaily wrapped packages and shouting to make themselves heard above the noise of gears changing and horns pooping. It would be another world.

Then he saw that some of the shops had entrances set back from the pavement. Just now these entrances were brilliant with light from the bright windows which flanked them. But he had imagination. He pointed.

'There. You see it standing there.' He could almost see it himself. When the shop windows were darkened there would be shadows which the street lights overhead wouldn't reach.

His father hadn't paid much attention to the pointing finger. 'In the shop?' he said, and laughed.

'In the doorway. You don't notice it at first. Not until you're walking right past, like we are now. And then you see. No. You don't see. You walk almost past, and then you feel.'

'Feel? What?'

'Just something. Cold.'

'Cold?'

'And you look sort of sideways. Without moving your head, because you don't want it to think you're really looking. But you do see it. Just standing. It doesn't move. Not then.'

'What does it look like? I suppose it's wearing armour. Has its head under its arm. Something like that?' the father said, willing to play along with the game.

'You don't see properly. Remember, it's dark. But it's partly because you're looking sideways, not straight at it. So you don't know exactly what it's like. You just have this feeling, that it's there because of you. Waiting for you.'

'I should walk past.'

'You do walk past. But then you start wondering. Whether there really was anything there.'

'I could always go back and have another look to make sure,' the father said.

'You'd never do that!' the boy said.

'Why wouldn't I?'

'Because you're frightened. You don't want to go back. You want to get away as quickly as you can.'

'Even though I'm not sure whether I saw anything or not?' the father asked.

'You hope you didn't, but really you know you did.'

'So I walk away, like we're walking now?'

'Only it's not like this. It's all quiet. There aren't any other people, or cars or anything. There's only you. And it, of course.'

'I could do without these crowds. Get on a bit faster,' the boy's father said.

'That's what you'd like to think,' the boy said.

'Why don't I, then?'

'Because you're listening all the time.'

'Listening what for?'

'The footsteps.'

'What do you mean, footsteps? If there aren't any other people.'

'*Its* footsteps. What you hope you didn't see.'

'Running after me?'

'Not running. Just walking, like you are. Not any faster, not catching up. You can't be sure you really hear them, because they're going the same pace as you, and if you stop, they stop too. You don't know if they're really there, or if it's just your own footsteps you're listening to.'

'I should turn round and have a look,' the father said.

'No.'

'Why not? That'd be the sensible thing to do.'

'You aren't feeling sensible,' the boy answered.

The father was tired of the game. He said, 'Hungry? What about some tea? They have crumpets at Jerningham's. We have to go there anyway to get the gear your Mum wants for icing the cake.'

They went through the swinging doors into the great lighted, jostling store, the high ceiling garlanded with paper chains, tinsel and holly twisted round the staircase rails and up the imitation marble pillars. A gilded cage shot them up five floors to the restaurant, and, sitting high above the sparkling streets, they drank hot, sweet, brown tea, and sucked the salty butter out of crumpets with as many holes in their pale faces as a sponge. At last, pleasantly full, licking the salt from their lips, they went down in the lift to the basement. There they searched for and found the gadget needed by the boy's mother, then mounted an escalator, reached the ground floor and fought their way through the crowd to the doors leading out into the street. By now the street lamps were lit. The shop windows blazed with an extra radiance. Behind the plate glass an assortment of objects was displayed to tempt last minute shoppers. But the boy hardly glanced at them. Most of them were grown-up things anyway. Who wanted to get a washing machine for a Christmas present? Or an armchair? It was stupid, too, to pretend that great big things like that could be wrapped in coloured paper and tied up with ribbons like a box of chocolates. His legs ached, and the heat of the big store had made him sleepy. He wouldn't have minded going home straight away. He pressed closer to his father's side.

'Where are we going now?' he asked.

'Got to get a bit of wood, fifty-four by ninety by five, for the shelf in the larder. Half a dozen cup-hooks and a tin of varnish. Might call in and see if Charlie at Deckers has got the beading I asked him for. That's all,' the father said.

They walked further along the crowded street to the builders' merchant, where the bit of wood, fifty-four by ninety by five should have been waiting, ready cut for them. But they had to wait. In the Christmas rush it had been stacked somewhere out at the back, no one was sure where. The boy sat on a chair by the high counter and looked, without really seeing, at all the tools arranged in precise order of their uses and graded in size, making patterns in the display on the opposite wall. He fumbled in the carrier bag he held, and found the carton of peppermint lumps which he'd bought earlier in the day. He unwrapped one and sucked it dreamily while he waited, thinking about nothing in particular, too tired even to be bored.

It was over an hour later when, the wood and the beading at last collected, the father and son began their return journey along the shopping street. And now everything had changed. The shoppers were all gone. The place had an empty, lost look. Tatters of coloured paper, lolly-sticks and bus tickets littered the pavements. A slight, cold rain was falling. Just now there were no buses on the road, and only the occasional car, the red rear lights looking like the eyes of some wild animal backing away from them along the deserted street.

They passed Jerningham's, alive only an hour ago with busy shoppers. Now the gilded doors were firmly shut, and inside the dim lights showed no movement, only the shapes of sheeted stands and counters, a shadowy emporium served by nothing but a skeleton staff. The man and the boy walked on, past more closed doors and windows, in which the lights were being, one by one, extinguished. They walked slowly, the man encumbered by the piece of wood under his arm and the parcels which dangled from his hand. The boy was tired; they had been out for a long time. He lagged behind, and his father called to him sharply.

'Get a move on, son. We don't want to take all day, do we?'

'I'm coming as fast as I can,' the boy said.

'Come on, then.'

As the father turned back to make for the bus station round the next corner, his glance fell across the window of the shop they were passing. In that split second he had the curious impression that a pair of eyes were regarding him steadily from behind the glass. Huge, dark eyes, as large as the eye sockets in a . . . He turned quickly to look more carefully, and saw that what he had mistaken for the fixed, sightless stare of a skull, was nothing but a pair of spectacles, suspended half way up the window by a thread which he hadn't seen in this half light. Reassured, he turned back once more, and by this time his stride, which had hardly faltered, had carried him past the window. Now he was level with the entrance to the shop itself, one of those deep entrances, the door set ten feet or so back from the pavement and flanked by the shrouded sides of the two windows. Somehow it seemed familiar, and at first he couldn't think why. Then he remembered. It was an entrance like this to which the boy had pointed, hours ago, during that silly conversation about ghosts. It could even have been this very one; he hadn't taken that much notice. But the memory was an uncomfortable one, and he felt a tiny shiver run down his spine. But that was ridiculous. Of course there would be nothing in the doorway that shouldn't be there, even where the shadows were blackest. Yet he felt an uneasy

50

reluctance to turn his head and to look directly in. Of course if he did, he would see that there was nothing there. But to feel obliged to look was silly ... childish. He really did not mean to look. But in spite of himself, his eyes slewed round just as he reached the further side of the entrance, his sight trying to penetrate that patch of densest darkness at the far end of the short passageway.

What happened next had nothing to do with his thinking self. It was the impulse of blind panic. Before he knew what he was doing, he had clutched the boy's wrist with his free hand, and he was running down the empty street, the unwieldy length of wood biting into his side, the parcels hanging from his wrist swinging against his thigh. His breath came in short, painful gasps, the fierce beating of his heart hammered in his ears. He felt deafened by its insistent pounding and yet through everything he could hear footsteps behind him. Not the lighter steps of his son, dragging at his hand, but heavier steps, measured with his own, echoing from the deserted pavement and from the blank, dead windows of the shuttered shops.

He checked himself at last at the corner of the big road, busy with cars, and with people pushing towards the bus station and the car park. Less than twenty yards away he could see the familiar shape of the red double-decker waiting for them, full of light and passengers. Many passengers, he was reassured to notice. He slowed to walking pace. He needed to recover his dignity. He shifted the awkward length of timber under his arm, released the boy's wrist and changed the hanging parcels to the other hand.

'Thought we were going to miss the bus,' he said.

'You hurt me. You almost pulled my arm out of its socket,' the boy complained as they joined the queue.

'Thought we were late,' the man said.

'There's another bus goes at seven. We could have got that,' the boy said. Then looking down, he said, reproachful, 'I've dropped my sweets. You made me drop my sweets. They were on top of my carrier bag, and now they're not there. They must've fallen out when you made me run like that.'

'Never mind. They don't matter,' his father said.

'I do mind. They cost thirty p,' the boy said.

'I'll give you the thirty p,' his father said.

'But it's a waste. We could go back and look for them. There's plenty of time. . . .'

'We're not going back,' the man said. He was shouting. The boy looked at him, surprised. The man said, more quietly, 'No point in going back. We'd better get on the bus.'

The boy followed his father, wondering, as he often did, at the way grown-up people behaved. Sometimes when you thought everything was all right, they got cross. Sometimes they laughed at what you said, when there wasn't anything funny about it. Now Dad shouted at him for nothing. You'd have thought he'd be pleased to save thirty p instead of getting het up at the idea of going back to look for the carton of sweets. He saw his father stow the length of wood and the larger parcels in the baggage space, and they climbed to the upper deck. The boy pushed into the window side of the seat. The man sat beside him, thankful for the chance to sit down in the light and in company. His legs were trembling – from the unaccustomed exercise, of course.

The bus ground its gears, inched out into the road and lumbered off away from the lighted streets of the town. Soon it was lurching along the unlit country roads, where the blackness was broken here and there by the yellow lights of cottage windows, and where giant skeleton trees loomed suddenly, scratching the windows of the upper deck with bony fingers, as if they might break through the glass and snatch the faces inside to carry them off to the sightless world without. The boy leaned against his father, going over in his mind the events of the afternoon. He thought of the presents he'd bought for his brother and small sister, of the handkerchiefs he'd got for Mum. He thought of the sweet rubbery flesh of the crumpets and of the soppy music they'd listened to while they ate their tea. He thought of the shops they'd passed earlier, while they were still brightly lit and he'd picked out things he'd have liked for himself in their windows. He thought of the conversation he'd had with his father there.

He said, drowsily, 'What would you really do if you saw a ghost, Dad?' It didn't surprise him that, in the usual grown-up way, his father didn't answer that properly. Instead he said, 'We had to catch this bus. Mum would have worried. She might have thought something had happened to us.'

The boy said, 'No, she wouldn't. She'd know we'd come back all right.'

Some quality in his father's silence made him repeat, 'She'd know we were all right. There isn't anything could happen to us. Could it, Dad?'

His father said, quickly, 'Of course not. What could happen to us?'

CATHERINE STORR

When the Grey Horses Trot

'Go on, Grandad.'
  'Go on.'
  'Go on, tell us.'
  'Tell us now.'
  'Go on.'
  'I said before—'
  'Aaaaaah, go on.'
  'Please.'
  'Ple–ease.'
  'I told you before, I'll tell you tonight, and I'll not tell you about it
till then, and that's that.'
  'Aaah—'
  'Now listen.' The old man raised his stick and pointed. 'Do you
see that wall down there, down behind them bushes? There's ivy on
it. D'you see it, Joanna?'
  'Yes—'
The girl stepped forward a pace and put her chin on the top bar of
the gate in front of her.
  'Phil?'
  'Yes. . . .'
  'That was a ganger's hut, that's what we call 'em. The men who
kept the line in working order used to go in there. Well – just you
remember it.'
  'Why?'
  'You'll find out. Can you see how the cutting just beyond it isn't so
steep? – It's so grown over I can hardly recognize it myself now. Do
you see it?'
  'Can't we go down there?' asked the boy.
  'Just to look?'
  'What did I tell you, Philip, eh?'

'Aaaah—'

'I said I'd bring you out and show you from a distance, didn't I? I wouldn't go down there now for all the tea in—'

'But, Grandad,' interrupted Joanna, 'we can hardly see anything from here.'

'Let's walk on a bit then.'

'This is better,' said the Grandfather, at the next gate.

From here they could see the old railway cutting clearly, a line of bushes and trees extending along the lowest point in the valley. It was a misty September day with a warm, clinging dampness in the air. To Joanna and Philip the old line below them looked dark and dank, and perhaps, a little forbidding.

'There it is,' said the Grandfather.

'The tunnel. Do you see, there, the bricks, where they blocked it up? There'll be a notice up saying it's dangerous to go inside. Not far wrong, either.'

'But *why's* it dangerous, Grandad?' asked Philip. 'It's only an old tunnel, isn't it?'

'I daresay it is only a tunnel – like a hundred others I've been through before and since.'

'So, what—'

'And do you see that field?' continued the old man.

'There beyond the line, where it's still up on the embankment just before it goes into the cutting. – And I'll be blowed if there isn't a horse in it now, and all!'

'Oh yes, I see the horse. Nice old horse, looks sleepy.'

'Well, you remember that field. Imagine, if you can, what it'd be like, riding past it in a loco down there, only with the telegraph wires up, and going by, whish – whish – whish. . . . Just try to picture that, for now.'

'All right . . .' said Joanna dubiously.

'Good. That's it then.'

'That's it?'

'That's all you need to see. Come on now. We'll get into trouble with your Mum if she finds I've brought you up here.'

The Grandfather made to move off, then paused.

'By gum,' he said, shaking his head sadly, 'you'd never think we used to run the locos along that strip of woodland down there. Might as well have been built by the Romans.'

It was a cool evening, and after dinner they lit a coal fire in the back room with its view over the one-time railway yard. The old man sat next to the fire with his mug of tea, and the children kneeled on the rug by his feet, expectant.

'I wonder what's on the telly tonight,' mused the Grandfather as he lit his pipe.

'Shall we have it on?'

'Oh, *no!*' cried both children, laughing.

'Tell us the *story*, Grandad!' Philip pulled off one of his grandfather's slippers. 'I won't give it back to you if you don't tell us!'

'Well . . .' said the old man, puffing on his pipe. 'Let me see. It's nearly six o'clock now. That's not so far off, is it? It was about seven o'clock it happened, on September fourteenth, fifty years ago tonight.' He spoke with exaggerated care, as if to reinforce the truth of what he was saying by clear diction. Then he glanced out of the window at the hazy yellow sky.

'I was twenty-four then, and I was still a fireman – I didn't do the driving, but I was second in command, like, and I had to look after the fire engine – anyhow my driver was a man named Tom McGee. Terrible Tom McGee, that was what he was known as.'

'Was that really his name?'

'Tom McGee was his name, yes. And he got called Terrible Tom McGee because – well, you know, there was something terrible about him. He was a big feller, well over six foot, and broad, and he was, like, all red to look at – bright red hair and a thick red bushy beard, right down here—' He held his hand nine inches under his chin.

'And he had great thick eyebrows, but they were black, and reddish hair all over his forearms, and under it you could see his tattoos, in blue – I remember one of them was of a rose, and another was a snake. . . . He had a very deep voice too. He was the kind of man that people respected straight off. They might not have liked him, but they respected him. That was one reason he was a driver, of course. He scared most of them, I do believe, including the bosses. He scared me, when I first worked with him. He hardly said a word to me, just gave me orders. So I didn't say anything either, and did my job as I was told. That's how it was in those days, of course, but with Tom McGee there was something extra to him over the other drivers. He wasn't just in charge. It was as if he was forbidding to people, as if no one *could* talk to him. Kept to himself when he was in the station. No stationmaster ever complained to him, as far as I can remember. And no one ever joked with him either. I don't remember ever seeing him smile – except once.'

At this point the children's mother, who had been washing up, came in with her apron still on and a dripping washing-up brush in her hand.

'You're not telling them that story, are you, Dad?' she asked.

'I am, Molly. Can you think of a better time than tonight?'

'But you'll scare them, Dad. And they won't believe you, either.'

'You believed me, didn't you? Now – where was I? There were rumours about Tom McGee, too. And there was one that may well have something in it, though how many of the fellers at work could have known for certain I can't say. Anyway, somehow it had got about that Tom McGee had once killed a man. They said he'd been wild when he was younger. He'd been in the Merchant Navy before he joined the railways. And there was this story about him, that when he'd been in Singapore one time he'd killed a trader there in an argument of some sort, he'd only hit him, but the man had died. And he'd been duly tried, and then acquitted, and released, just like that. Well, I didn't pay too much attention to this story until one day he said something to me which seemed – but only seemed – to tie up with it.'

'What did he say?' asked Philip, snuggling against his grandfather's leg.

'Wait, lad, wait. Anyhow, you might guess that this story didn't make it any easier for the fellers at the station to be fraternal with Tom McGee. "I hear you're working with Tom McGee now. Take care, lad," one of them told me, "and especially you take care when you work with him on the Thixendale line." I asked him what he meant, of course, but all he'd say was that he couldn't explain. He said, "There's nothing to explain. But just you mark my words, and take care."

'Well now,' continued the Grandfather. 'Tom McGee's locomotive was called the *Ravenham Hall.* She was a great beauty, and you had to hand it to him, McGee loved that engine more than many loved their wives. He cared for it above and beyond the call of duty. They were all very proud in those days, the drivers. We presented ourselves well, you understand. Not like nowadays! And the drivers, they'd clean up their engines themselves, and they'd go out, many of them, on their days off and clean 'em and polish 'em, like your Mum polishes her best cutlery, and the *Ravenham Hall* she always looked a treat. It was almost as if McGee's engine was a part of himself.'

The old man paused to relight his pipe, puffing one little cloud of smoke after another out of the corner of his mouth.

'But what happened to Terrible Tom McGee, Grandad?'

'And what about the tunnel?'

'Patience, patience. You don't tell a story by getting to the end before you've half begun it. Now. The first time I worked with Tom McGee I decided very quick how it was going to be with him. He said very little to me, so I thought, I'll say even less, unless he asks me something. I never gave him cause to complain to me – I never would have done with any driver, but I think I tried that bit harder with him. And Tom McGee was a good driver. Never got nervous at the level crossings like some drivers do. I have done myself, because accidents do happen at level crossings, a lorry stuck across the line, or some cattle. But he blew his whistle, and went straight through like a flash.

'But then, one day, we had to do the Thixendale line. When I heard I thought "Aye aye, now for it." I was ready and waiting, as it were, though what for I had not the faintest idea. Well, we rolled out of Malton, and we stopped at Langston Halt and picked some passengers up at Burythorpe, and that was all right. It was a fine, clear summer day if my memory does not deceive me, and the air was warm, one of those days when you get up a sweat stoking before you've hardly started. And the country looked beautiful, all the little villages and church towers going past, and the animals in the fields. . . .

'In half an hour we were climbing up to the Wolds, and there were no more halts or stations then before Thixendale itself which is, of course, on the other side of the tunnel I showed you this morning. A clear run, all the way. The line climbs – climbed, I should say – into a valley, and then it levels out and there's around a mile of flat, most of it downhill, before the tunnel itself, you could get on quite a bit of speed, if need be. We got to the beginning, and rode along fine. But it was then that I noticed that Tom McGee was staring, right out of the cab. Now if you're a driver that's something you never do, or not for more than a moment. You've got to keep your eye on the line. Anything might happen. You've got to be prepared. But there he was, staring and staring over to the right and ahead – as if he was expecting something. And I saw that he was getting nervous, drumming his fingers and – it's difficult to pin it down, you know, especially after all these years. But he was like a rock, that Tom McGee, at every other time, and yet here he was now getting right het up and I could not for the life of me imagine what about. There was nothing there, only fields, like you saw. Then we went into the cutting, the one I showed you, and down past the ganger's hut, and it was as if he was a balloon that had got let down or something, all the tension went out of him, and we rode on into the tunnel, he whistled, and—'

The old man paused to fumble for his matches in his cardigan pocket.

'*What*, Grandad!'

'Oh, we went through. We went straight through, and got to Thixendale spot on time. Not a hitch, that time. Where's me matches gone?'

'They're down the side of the seat, Dad,' said Molly who was still there, and listening too.

'Oh yes. Can't tell a story without me pipe. Makes me nervous you know. Well, anyhow, that was the first time, and of course after that I was prepared. The next time was a week later, as I remember. I didn't say nothing to anyone in the meantime – well, what was there to say? But come the day before the run I was as jittery as a cat in a dog's home. I kept saying to myself "You've not cause to be, you've no cause at all," but it didn't help much. Anyhow, the time came and we were off, and I was watching him. By! I was watching him, and I was watching out for whatever it might be that he was staring after, too. This time I could see how he grew tense – it was just the same – and how he began to fidget with his hands as we came along the valley. I kept my eye fixed on that view of the cab, but for the life of me I could see nothing new, nothing unusual at all out there. Trees, fields, one with some horses in it. Six horses there were – six grey horses. And then, I don't know how it came to me but somehow I twigged on it – it was *them*, the horses, he was looking after. One of them did something, nothing much, pawed the ground with a foreleg maybe, and Tom McGee he gripped that handle like he was going to squeeze it into a new shape. But then, it was as if he sensed that I'd been watching him, and he looked round at me – and truly there was something terrible in his eyes then, so I could imagine only too well how he'd come to be called Terrible Tom McGee.'

'Were they magic horses?' asked Joanna.

The old man laughed a wheezy laugh, and reflected a moment.

'Magic horses,' he repeated. 'I've thought about that myself, once or twice. No, the horses weren't magic. I don't think so. They were just ordinary horses that happened always to be in the same field.

'The next thing I learned was purely by accident. I might never have known anything that could be explained to make any kind of sense, but for this. I was coming home late one night, and I cut across the yard out there, as I sometimes did instead of going the long way round, and blow me if I didn't bump right smack into Tom McGee, and bump into him is right because he was blind drunk. Rolling, he was, and I could tell straight away, before he said a word, that he was miserable with it. You get that, you know, when two men work together a long time. They may not say much to one another but they get very alert to each other's moods. And that's how it had become with me and him. He nearly fell on me, tripped on a sleeper maybe, and he swore when he realized I was there, but then he saw it was me and he grabbed me by the lapel and looked me hard in the eye. And he said to me "That tunnel, lad. That tunnel!" It was, you know, as if he had been keeping it to himself too long and now he *had* to talk to someone, under any circumstances. Maybe he'd been brooding on it all night, I don't know, and drinking himself silly, and then he'd bumped into me – and he knew that I knew – that I knew something anyway. He said to me, "You saw the horses, didn't you?" so I said "Yes, I saw them." Just like that, I couldn't lie to Tom McGee – show me the man that could! "They're always there," he says, "always have been there. Always will be—" and his eyes wandered away from me around the sidings and the rolling stock. "You saw how they were grazing, didn't you?" I nodded. "Well one day they aren't going to be grazing. One day they'll run, you listen to me now—" he breathed hard on me and his breath stank of rum, "and when those horses trot together, as one day I know they will do – I know, you see – then that tunnel will not go through the hill to Thixendale but it will open up and take the engine, and me with it, down to the bowels, lad, down to the bowels! For that tunnel is a tunnel to Hell, lad, and it's a-waiting for me."

'So that was it. Well, what was I to do, with McGee jamming me up against a wagon with his great meaty fist clapping a tight hold on my lapel? I was speechless. What he said, it seemed to drop right into place and make sense, and then again it made no sense at all. He let go of me, in time, and looked down at the ground, and said in a croaking, hoarse voice "I must pay, you see. I must pay." What for, and why, and how he came to think it – these are things that neither I nor anyone else will ever know for certain now, though we may guess. But think it he did. Think it! He was crazy with it.

'I tried to decide he was mad. But then, what if he was? A mad engine driver, and me his fireman? That's a pretty kind of a pickle to find yourself in. So, I thought, maybe I should report the incident, go over his head. But what if he denied it, and they believed him, being my superior? So I did nothing. But there was another reason for saying nothing, too, I have to confess it – and that was that in a funny kind of way I almost believed him myself. Despite myself, like.

'The next time we went up,' he continued as the light faded in the room about them, 'we avoided one another's eyes. Quite deliberate, it was. We went about our business, but with a kind of an extra show of efficiency. He was surly, and very efficient with it. I can't remember our speaking once. We got to the valley, and I saw him tensing up as I knew he would. Over and over I'd say to myself, "It's nonsense. Do your job and ignore it. It's nonsense", and now I was saying it like a chant, in time with the noise from the engine. And I thought, "Here it comes, old mad McGee's moment of fear", trying to put it outside myself, to convince myself it was just *him*. But it wasn't just him, you see. I found that I wasn't watching him, I was watching out of the cab, waiting for the field with the horses, with my heart in my mouth. And then there it was, and there they were, and one walked this time and I found I was broken out in a cold sweat at the sight of a horse walking! Then we were past, and the tunnel was coming at us, over us, and the engine rattled and roared through the dark, and then we were out the other side, and coming down almost before I could realize it, coming down to Thixendale station. When we'd got in and halted, Tom McGee he turned to me and blow me if he didn't give me a knowing smile. And blow me if I didn't find myself smiling back!'

The old man laughed quietly to himself at this.

'So then,' he continued, 'we came by and by to the evening of the fourteenth of September.

'. . . And by the time that evening came about I had decided once and for all that Tom McGee was mad. We'd been through that tunnel many times, but each time nothing happened, and each time I got more certain of myself. What was I doing believing this madman? I'd end up in a padded room myself, if I kept on that way! One day the farmer was going to move those horses to another field – I'd even thought of going to ask him myself – and then old McGee'd be in trouble. Then he'd have to find something else to scare himself with. Cows, I thought, or chickens maybe, signalling the way to Hell. So, that evening I got up into the cab very calm and collected. And there we were, riding out of Malton on a goods run, with six wagon-loads of sheep. I was very calm, watching old McGee, waiting for him to get nervous. Maybe he did, I can't be sure, but he

63

didn't *seem* half as fidgety this time as on earlier runs. He stared out of the cab as he always did, and even now, completely against my reasoning, mind, I found my eyes wandering that way too. I'd come to recognize the field by now, there was one with barley in it, the next one with cattle, another empty one dotted with old oaks, and then there it was, the field with the horses and they were almost below us this time, right by the line. . . .

'Maybe it was a spark or two from the engine, but anyway something startled them, and I watched them as if they were moving in slow motion, or under water, as they began, all six of them, to gallop away up the field. Beautiful they were, with their grey manes streaming out, and as I watched, in a kind of daze I must have been, I think I also heard a great cry – like a cry, I can't say exactly, but almost of triumph – from Tom McGee. Not a cry of fear, mind, it wasn't that. Before I could so much as breathe he had the shovel out of my hands and he was hurling the coal into the furnace. He wanted it you see, he *wanted* it! I cannot ever forget the picture I have of him then, lit red by the flames of the fire, his hair, and the hair on his arms, redder than red in that light and his eyes burning – like the coal in that grate there. Then he threw down the shovel and had me by the collar and belt, and I found myself flying through the air. He'd flung me out of the cab! I hit some bushes. If I hadn't, I'd've been a hospital case ever after. That ganger's hut I showed you was right by me – if I'd hit that I'd've been dead – and the train was going past, the sheep all baaing away in the wagons. As fast as I could I scrambled up, but I didn't see the train go into the tunnel. I heard it after. I heard the whistle go, and go, and go, and I heard it echo down the tunnel, and it seemed to turn into a bigger echo, and yet bigger. It was as if the train had not gone into the tunnel, but into some enormous cave. Then there was nothing. No clattering of wheels, no engine sound, just silence. I stood there, a bit bruised but otherwise unhurt, at a loss for what to do. Then I heard, or fancied I heard – the whistle for the last time, and the sound seemed to come from a great, great distance, from far further away than the valley at Thixendale and from deep down, almost as if it was coming . . . from the bowels of the earth. And that did indeed prove to be the end of terrible Tom McGee and the *Ravenham Hall.*'

'They disappeared?'

'Aye. They did not come out the other side of that tunnel. You can see the newspaper cuttings, if you want. "Entire Train Vanishes

with Driver." "Company Officials Baffled at Missing Train Mystery." All that kind of thing. There's even one that says McGee stole the engine! I suppose in a way he did. Have you ever heard the phrase, "You can't take it with you"? Tom McGee took a whole locomotive with him – wherever he went. The line continued to be used, of course, until it was closed by Dr Beeching. With no further incidents, I might add.'

'Did you use it, Grandad?'

'Er – no, Joanna. No, I didn't.'

'Were you scared to?'

'I was. Wouldn't you have been? The one question, though, that's stuck in my mind all these years is – was he right? I mean, in thinking that he would go to Hell. You see, for all his strange character, he didn't seem a bad man to me, Tom McGee. And if you look at what he did, chucking me out like that, he was doing me a favour, wasn't he, in his terms? A wicked man wouldn't have bothered, I reckon. And if he hadn't've bothered, God knows where I'd be now! I hoped he was wrong – and not just for his sake, either – I always think of those sheep he took with him. They were off to the canning factory, as I remember, and that's a pretty poor choice to be given, isn't it, Hell or the Irish Stew?'

GARETH LOVETT JONES

Exit

'Come on,' said Hawkins eagerly, in his piping voice. 'Let's get off at the Post Office. We can soon walk up there.'

'In this?'

Carter gazed out doubtfully, as the bus rocketed along the empty road. Every now and then a few fat drops of rain fell out of a yellowish sky and dashed against the window. Beyond the hedges the fields, caught in the strange light, showed a living, incandescent green.

'Go on, be a sport. Come with me, will you? This is practically *ideal*.'

It wasn't the sort of weather most people would have called ideal. The storm had been brewing all day, with thunder rolling in the distance. What Hawkins meant was 'ideal for him', i.e. ideal for trying out his theory.

'Come on,' said Hawkins again, getting agitated, 'we're nearly there.'

'Oh, all right,' Carter said then, out of good nature.

They grabbed up their school bags and Hawkins rang the bell. The bus stop served a few cottages and a farm a little way up the hill. One of the cottages was also a Post Office. Opposite the Post Office a track led up a gentle slope to a ruined chapel – their destination.

They crossed the road – there was hardly ever any traffic – and set off up the hill, rather clumsy and heavy-footed on the stones of the muddy path. They were laughing and larking about as they walked along.

'What exactly are you hoping to see?' said Carter. 'If hoping is the right word.'

'I'm not sure. Monks, white ladies, something like that.'

'What about the old nameless dread, eh?'

'That too.'

The path narrowed and they got into single file. They hadn't far to go. The chapel was only a field or two away from the road, in a small wood fenced off – inadequately – with barbed wire. You could actually see the decayed end wall from the bus, if you looked at the right moment. All the same, close to civilization though it was, it had somehow succeeded in keeping its own peculiar atmosphere.

To his surprise, Carter found his mood changing: all his jokiness was dropping away: a feeling of oppression sat heavily in his chest. He wasn't going to let on to Hawkins, though. He decided it must be the weather. It was the queerest weather, so heavy and overcast. Thunder rumbled again. It was getting nearer.

'Listen to that!' continued his friend, still in the same loud tones. 'We should see something. Or it could be we'll just feel a drop in the temperature.'

Carter wished he'd let him come on his own. There wasn't all that much of a friendship between them: they just travelled in the same direction from school, and usually caught the same bus home. They weren't even in the same year. Hawkins was a clever little squirt out of Form Two, all specs and long words. Carter was older and brawnier. When they sat on the bus together Hawkins liked to rattle on, and Carter, who was good-natured, let him. He wasn't much of a talker himself. Hawkins was always full of ideas.

'Tell me it again,' said Carter, out of a dryish throat, 'your idea.'

They were nearly at the wood.

'It's simple, really,' piped Hawkins, importantly. It wasn't simple at all, except at the start. 'My theory is, there is some connection between thunderstorms and psychic phenomena. You know that photograph I showed you out of the library – that one with the ghostly shape on it? That was taken at Corfe Castle just before a thunderstorm.'

'Bet it was a fake.'

'Maybe,' said Hawkins with scientific open-mindedness.

'And anyway – it wasn't taken here.'

'No, but it was in this sort of a place, a well-known spooky spot. Even if that one was a fake, it doesn't really matter. The point is, there are so many accounts of apparitions and hauntings connected with storms, there must be something in it.'

'I wouldn't have thought you believed in ghosts.'

Hawkins shrugged. 'Well, I don't believe in ghosts, exactly. What

I really think is, *either* something in the past leaves a sort of photograph, or film of itself, quite by accident, which you can pick up when the atmosphere's right; *or* – this is my other theory' – he paused impressively – 'beings *from other worlds* reach through to us here. Whichever it is, it's connected with these special places, and storms.'

'*Other worlds?*'

'Yes. You know, out of deep space, or another time – what do you call it – an alternative universe. You see, if people here happened to see something like that, they'd naturally interpret it as a ghost, or the devil, or something supernatural, wouldn't they?'

Carter stood still, apparently to get his breath. 'You mean *we* might see things from outer space.'

'Lots of people have – UFOs and all that – they're always seeing them in Wales. Or we might see a funny sort of historical film, if my first theory's correct. Boy! If there is anything here, this is the day to see it.' He hurried eagerly up the last few yards of the path. Carter followed, slowly.

'Hawkins, what are you *supposed* to see here?'

'Dunno. I just know that it has this reputation for being haunted.'

It was easy getting into the wood. The wire had rusted through in places. There was a strong scent of bluebells everywhere; they were almost over, dying mostly. You couldn't walk without treading on them.

'Nothing stirring yet,' said Hawkins. In the wood even he sounded subdued, as if he had suddenly realized what in fact he might see. Carter moved his shoulders uneasily: it was a curious animal uneasiness, purely physical. He had not believed a word Hawkins had said.

They went on towards the chapel. Most of its grey stones had been carted away years ago, but the foundations and one wall remained. The thunder sounded again, but it seemed further off now.

'Well, this is it.' There was a quaver in Hawkins's voice, and he jumped when a spatter of rain fell on him. A raindrop ran like a tear down his glasses. And then he disappeared.

Suddenly, and with great completeness, Hawkins was no longer there. Carter had been staring right at him, even noticing the yellow streak of light reflected in his glasses and the splosh of rain. The light had touched the wall too, just above his friend's head.

Wait. It was at this point that the blood in Carter's veins chilled to ice water, and that each hair rose separately on his head and arms.

There was *no wall.* He turned round. There were no trees, no electric pylons, no cottages, no road. The lie of the land was not the same. There was no storm. The sky was clear, a curious pale mauve colour. There was no sun. He was standing alone in a rocky place, and a small wind was blowing. A wild facetiousness swept over him. He started to laugh. *He* was the one who had disappeared. Exit. Finis. Out goes he.

Then he burst into tears. 'That Hawkins, when I get hold of him, I'll kill him. I'll duff him up. I'll make him wish he'd never been born.'

Of course, he was never able to do any of these things.

PATRICIA MILES

Mr Hornet and Nellie Maggs

'No, Denis, I am *not* always picking on you,' said Mr Hornet, in his high thin voice that seemed to come from the back of his nose. 'It is just that I take you as I find you, and I find you . . .' Mr Hornet paused, lightly tapping a ruler on the grubby exercise book before him until he had the full attention of the class, '. . . repulsive.'

The class tittered politely, and Mr Hornet continued, rocking back on his heels, 'Do you know what repulsive means, Denis?'

'Nope.'

Mr Hornet glanced round the waiting pack. 'Can anyone kindly enlighten our Denis?'

A forest of hands shot up. They might not be too sure about 'repulsive', but they knew Mr Hornet, and they knew Denis. Each awaited the teacher's nod.

'Nasty, sir.'

'Dirty.'

. 'Untidy.' This was felt to be a weak contribution, and the class gathered itself to do better.

'Turns you off, sir.' Somebody in the opposite corner made a realistic vomiting noise. Now the hunt was up.

'Picks his nose.'

'Pongs, sir.'

'Tells lies.'

Suddenly Emma was on her feet, from the row in front of Denis, three desks along. Her neck was flushed crimson under the mane of ginger hair, and she held her arm high as she stood very straight and still. Mr Hornet could not ignore her. 'Emma?'

'Sad, sir.'

One or two children giggled at Emma for having missed the point of the game, and someone tried to bring her in line by saying, 'Yeah, miserable as sin.' But Emma stood there, spear-straight and fiery, while the joke fizzed about the classroom like a punctured balloon and dropped, a tattered shred, to the floor. Then she sat down.

In the silence that followed, Denis squinted sideways at her as he sat with head sunk low over grimy knuckles, but she never looked at him. If she had, he would have killed her or, worse, cried.

For some reason, he started thinking about Nellie Maggs.

Nellie lived in one of a pair of roadside cottages on the edge of town, out beyond the gas-works and the last filling station. Denis lived in the other one, with his half-brother, Mark, and Mark's wife and three-year-old daughter. There was another baby expected soon.

Nellie Maggs was going to be seventy next birthday. She had something wrong with her hips, that made her heave her body from side to side, like a duck, only she didn't move her legs fast like a duck, but slowly, as though each leg had to be thought about in turn before it would move. She had greyish-white hair, which she tucked in straggling wisps behind her big ears, and a wide, wide mouth. Her face was darker than her hair, and blotched, the colour of a light-brown frog and when her great grin broadened her face, that was exactly what she looked like, a kind, cheerful ugly frog.

Denis could not remember his mother at all, because she had only stayed with his father for a couple of years, and then gone off. No wonder, people had said, for Denis's father, apart from being twice her age, was well-known as the local drunk. When Denis was about eight, his father, weaving his way home from the pub, had stepped in front of a car pulling out from the filling station. There had been a funeral, and Mark had married Tracy, who came from a nice clean respectable family. Mark had been careful during the years he had been courting her never to bring her back to the cottage while his disreputable old father was alive, but now she moved in and quickly turned the old place into a spotless copy of her parents' home. Only Denis remained as a shabby reminder of the old days.

For most of his childhood, when no one else was around to look after the little Denis, Nellie Maggs had done it. She used to sit him on her crippled knees and read him fairy stories.

Denis stirred in his school desk, remembering the occasion which, looking back, marked the end of the bright days of childhood. It was when he was first conscious of being laughed at.

Nellie Maggs was reading him a story. '"What, kiss an ugly old frog like you?" screamed the princess. And she threw the poor frog across the floor,' read Nellie Maggs. Denis could still see the bright pictures and the pattern of print on the book that told the story of the princess who kisses the ugly frog to gain a wish, and turned the frog into a handsome prince.

'So now you know what you must do, my lovey, when you want something. Just you find the ugliest old frog you can, and give it a lovely big kiss.'

Denis had stared up at the leathery brown cheek a few inches from his face, and then he had flung his arms round her neck and kissed her, just by the bristly wart on her chin.

He hadn't minded when she cackled with laughter; but he minded the way his father laughed, and Mark, and Tracy, as the story was passed around for their amusement. It had even caught up with him at school, years later.

Life from then on seemed to be full of mockery. His father mocked him for being frightened and running to Nellie Maggs when he was drunk; Mark mocked him for being stupid; later Tracy mocked him. 'Denis, don't eat so disgusting.' 'Denis, wash your hands.' 'Didn't your father teach you nothing?' And at school it was all mockery.

Since Nellie Maggs was the only person who didn't seem to despise him, Denis could take a little comfort that she, at least, was a lower creature than he was. 'That old witch,' Mark called her, and Tracy was always afraid that germs would seep through from next-door, but when Denis started calling her 'That old witch' too, he got scolded for it. Once he tagged on to a gang of boys who threw stones through her windows and ran away. Emma, he thought, would not have done *that*. . . .

The end of afternoon school arrived, and Denis was just leaving the classroom when Mr Hornet called him back. 'You can wait, Denis, till the rest of the class has gone.'

'Oh, thanks,' muttered Denis, under his breath. The mean old devil. But then, old Hornet always had it in for him, just as the rest of his class had. Dregs, the other children called him. Not Denis the Menace, like other Denises. Just Dregs. When Mr Hornet beckoned him to come up to the teacher's desk, he shambled slowly forward.

'I've got something for you,' said Mr Hornet. He was feeling down inside his breast pocket, and came out with a tiny box. It appeared to have been home-made out of cardboard, about the size of a sugar-lump, and all bandaged up with sticky tape. It looked as if it had been in Mr Hornet's pocket for a long time, for bits of fluff and dirt clung to it.

'In this box,' said Mr Hornet, 'I have one happy day.'

Denis stared at him blankly. Then little threads of thoughts, like worms, began to wriggle in from the fringes of his mind. Was Hornet going mad? Was *he* mad? Or had he not been listening properly, and Mr Hornet had actually said something quite different? But the obvious things, like lines or detention, didn't come in sticky boxes the size of a sugar lump. For the box was there, in Mr Hornet's fingers, which were trembling as he tried to tear off the sticky tape.

'Scissors,' said Mr Hornet. 'Or a knife. Oh, quick!' He sounded as cross as usual, and in a tearing hurry, but scared, too, as though he might not be able to go through with whatever he had decided to do.

Denis had neither, but he produced his old bent compasses, and Mr Hornet managed to stab and wrench at the tape till he had slit one side open, jabbing his finger in the process so that the blood oozed out. Denis suddenly felt frightened at the thought that he was alone in the classroom with a madman armed with a pair of compasses. Ignoring that, Mr Hornet shook something out into the palm of his hand and held it out for Denis to see.

It was a small roundish object, rather like a pearl, only a bright, glowing red, semi-transparent, so that one could see a pinprick of gold glimmering and flickering away right in the heart of it.

'There,' said Mr Hornet, 'one happy day.'

'Pardon?' said Denis.

'Now listen carefully,' said Mr Hornet, and for once Denis did. Surprise had blown his mind clear of all its usual layers of fluff, and he remembered every word that Mr Hornet said for the rest of his life. 'When I put this jewel, or seed, into your hand, it will turn into two. One you swallow, and it will give you one perfectly happy day. The other one you must keep and give to someone else, just as I am giving you this one now, and just as somebody once gave one to me.'

What a funny thing to give to Mr Hornet, Denis thought. He must have been given it in the school holidays, because he's never had a happy day in school, to my certain knowledge. Bad-tempered, mean old creature, always.

'Why me?' he asked. Why, indeed. Mr Hornet had never tried to disguise his contempt for Denis. Perhaps it was all a trick to poison him.

'Because you need it,' said Mr Hornet. 'Now take it, quick, before I change my mind.'

Denis thought there could not be any harm in just holding it in his hand. That way he could see if it really turned into two, like Mr Hornet had said.

He held out his open hand and Mr Hornet took the pearl-like thing between his finger and thumb and placed it carefully in Denis's grimy palm. At once it began to roll about, hither and thither, like a live thing, in the small cup of his hand, too fast for the eye to follow the movement; only the colour danced in his hand, red and gold, bright as a flame, but without heat. Gradually the dancing colours slowed and settled, and in the palm of his hand lay two identical red-gold pearls.

Mr Hornet gave a great sigh. The tenseness and irritability went out of him and he smiled. 'Ah!' he said. Then he put a friendly hand on Denis's shoulder. 'Run along now,' he said, 'as soon as you have swallowed one of them. Then you'll have your happy day tomorrow.'

'Tomorrow's a school day,' said Denis. How could he have a happy day at school?

Mr Hornet was still unaccountably smiling. 'Your happy day will look after itself,' he said, 'but I don't suppose it will include school. If you just turn up again on Thursday, I shan't ask any questions about tomorrow.'

Denis looked at the two little objects in his hand. 'Why can't I swallow both, and have two happy days?' he said. One didn't seem much, out of a lifetime.

'You can,' said Mr Hornet. 'But then that's the end of it. You see, it only doubles when you give it to someone else. The great mistake – I see it now – is hanging on to the second one too long. You must give it to someone else who needs it – don't wait, like I did, for years and years. Now, just swallow the one and keep the other safe.'

'It's not poison, is it?' Mr Hornet looked so friendly that Denis felt able to ask the question and trust the answer.

'No,' said Mr Hornet, 'and it's not a drug, either. The things you'll do on your happy day will be real things, not just dreams.'

'It sounds like magic,' said Denis.

'Yes,' said Mr Hornet. 'That's what it is. You get half the magic tomorrow, and the rest later.'

Denis swallowed the pearl. It did not taste of anything in particular, nor did it make him feel any different. Mr Hornet gave him the comic little box for the second pearl, and found some more sticky tape to fasten it with. 'Don't lose it,' he said. 'Have a happy time tomorrow, and I'll see you in school on Thursday.' And he trotted jauntily off down the school staircase, humming a tune.

Denis fell asleep that night dreaming of all the things he would like to do on his happy day. They included a car chase, a shoot-out in a sewer and another in a multi-storey garage, foiling single-handed a plot to blow up the world and being a boy-emperor on horseback, leading his army into battle.

He was woken early by Mark coming in to say the baby was about to arrive and he was taking Tracy into hospital and dropping the three-year-old at her grandmother's. 'I won't get back till late tonight,' said Mark. 'Here's two quid for you to go to the pictures and get yourself something to eat.'

As soon as they had gone, Denis dressed, had breakfast and went to the railway station. There was a poster saying 'Take a rail trip to Biddleton-by-Lea and visit the County Show'. There were pictures of shire horses with arched necks and ribbons in their tails, motorcyclists flying through fiery hoops, vintage cars and a fairground.

Denis went to the ticket office. 'Half return to Biddleton,' he said.

'Two pounds exactly,' said the clerk, and flicked out the ticket. 'You're early. Hoping for a job there?'

'Yeah,' said Denis.

'I've got an uncle, has a farm there. They're always desperately busy the morning of the Show, getting stock ready. I used to help there myself when I was a kid. Good fun it was, too. When you come out from the station, don't take the road into town. Turn left – it's about half a mile up the lane. Say Joe sent you.'

'I will,' said Denis. 'Thanks.'

If the red pearl made magic, it made very business-like magic, Denis thought as he sat on the little train bustling out into the rich June countryside.

He found the farm without trouble. There was a magnificent shire horse, big as an elephant, tied up in the yard. A frisky colt was cavorting about on the end of a rope. 'Steady, steady now,' called the farmer, but the colt wasn't interested in being steady.

Seeing Denis hovering about in the yard the farmer said 'Looking for a job?'

'Yes, please. Joe sent me.'

'Get up on that horse, then, and carry on plaiting the mane from where I had to leave off. Not afraid of horses, are you?'

'No,' said Denis. He had never thought about it, but the horse looked as steady as a rock. He climbed on to a wall, and so on to the horse's back. It was warm and solid. He studied the way the red ribbon interlaced the shining black mane, and set to work. His fingers had an unaccustomed nimbleness.

'Oh, bless you,' said the farmer's wife, hurrying through the yard. 'You're as welcome as the birds in spring. Black Diamond trusts you. You've got good hands with a horse, I can see that.'

'You've made a tidy job of that,' said the farmer, when he had done. 'Now, can you polish up his coat till he shines like his name – Black Diamond?'

'I'll try,' said Denis. When it was time to set off with him to the showground everybody said what a good job Denis had done.

'You'll have to lead him round the ring,' said the farmer. 'After all the work you've put into him. I reckon we've got a good chance of a medal this year, a very good chance. Anyways, I shall have my hands full with the colt.'

So Denis led Black Diamond round and round the Judging Ring. He watched the other competitors carefully to know what to do, and walked so that the judges could admire the horse's stately tread, the great feathery feet that never trod on Denis's toes, and the corded muscles of the arched neck. Then he ran, and Black Diamond lifted his knees so that his feet rose up and down like pistons, and the plumes nodded above his great gentle head.

'First Prize to Black Diamond,' said the judges, so then Denis had to lead Black Diamond at the head of all the animals in the show right round the big ring for the Grand Parade.

Afterwards, he sat on the grass with the farmer's family, for he felt like one of them now, and ate bacon sandwiches and lettuce and huge slices of cream-filled sponge cake and strawberries, and washed it all down with cider. 'Thanks a lot, son,' said the farmer, afterwards, and gave him a five-pound note. 'Go and enjoy yourself now – but if ever you want a job on a farm, you know where to come. I shall expect you next year, mind!'

Even five pounds does not last for ever when there is so much to spend it on, and eventually Denis found himself standing by the bumper cars with not a penny left.

'Hey, you,' said the man in charge. 'I seen you in the Grand Parade. You seem a sensible lad. Could you take over from Charlie here while he goes and gets a bite to eat?'

Charlie's job was to take the money from the passengers in the bumper cars, and to help any of them who got stuck. Denis had noticed that he also gave himself free trips if one of the cars happened to be empty.

'Yeah, O.K.,' he said. He soon learnt how to climb across from car to car and sort out traffic jams, or disconnect a car that had failed and steer it to the side, and how to operate the emergency lever to bring everyone to a halt in an emergency. Things were pretty busy, because it was evening by now, and children had been out of school long enough to come from quite far away.

'Hullo!' said a voice. 'How did you get this job?' It was Emma, with her four-year-old brother. Denis gave them the car he knew went best, but after a while he saw they were in trouble, because two boys were making a dead set at Emma's car, deliberately crashing into it again and again. The little brother was getting frightened, and crying, and Emma was looking like crying, too, for she could not protect her brother from the jolts and steer the car as well. Denis leapt across the moving cars.

'You stop that!' he shouted. 'It's not allowed.' But they were bigger than him, and did not stop. Denis went and pulled the lever, and everything stopped. 'Out, you two,' he said, in the sudden silence. The boys were startled, and looking round saw the man in charge, a big burly fellow, coming over to see what was up. They leapt from the car and ran off among the crowds. Denis pulled the lever once more and the cars burst into life again.

'Quite right, sonny,' said a fat woman nearby. 'They didn't ought to be allowed to do that.'

'They can't while I'm around,' said Denis.

When Charlie came back, the man in charge gave Denis a free pass to go on all the things in the fairground. It enabled him to go on the flying boats with Emma, who was afraid to go by herself with her little brother, because he needed to have someone on each side of

him to keep him safe. He lent his free pass to the brother to go on the tiny ones' train, and they watched him go round and round while Denis licked the candy floss that Emma bought him in exchange.

Then Emma had to go home, but Denis went to watch the motorbike-racing.

Suddenly, just as the machines came skidding round the corner towards their part of the ring, a toddler staggered out from under the rail and tottered, giggling and unsteady, straight into the paths of the cyclists. Quick as lightning, Denis slipped out after him, and raced to pick him up. There was no time to run back with him; all he could do was stand quite still, clutching the child and let the machines roar past him on either side. A frantic father rushed out to meet him as he returned.

'It's all right,' said Denis, nonchalantly, and disappeared into the crowd. A little later, he heard the voice over the loudspeaker asking for the boy whose quick thinking had saved a child's life to come to the commentary box so that they could announce his name and give him a reward.

Denis was about to go, but then he stopped. He had been so happy all day he didn't need any reward. He'd been treated so kindly by so many people he didn't want any more fuss. It was time for the last train home, and he went quietly off and caught it.

Next day was awful, despite the fact that Mr Hornet continued that day and every day to be kind and cheerful, quite unlike his own self. Despite, too, Emma's tale to her friends of how she had met Denis at Biddleton Show and he'd been quite different from the Dregs they all knew at school. All that Denis could think about was that he had had his happy day and he would never have another. Unless, that is, he swallowed the other red pearl, and finished the chain of happiness for good, for the sake of one more happy day.

He could neither bring himself to do that, nor give it away, so he just went on being miserable, and scruffy, and ashamed, day after day after day. Anyway, he couldn't think whom to give it *to*. Someone who needed it, Mr Hornet had said. That ruled out Emma. There wasn't anyone else he wanted to make happy.

The new baby at home made matters worse. The little house was always full of bottles and nappies and squawling infant, and the three-year-old was always demanding attention, not wanting to be left out. One evening, Denis was driven to revive an old habit, and go round to watch television at Nellie Maggs. He had scarcely spoken to her since the stone throwing incident but he supposed she would welcome him with the usual wide grin.

He found Nellie Maggs lying on her back among the pansies, with tear-drops in the wrinkles of her cheeks.

'Nellie! Are you hurt?'

'Oh, Denis, lovey, thank God you've come. No, I'm not hurt – just overbalanced, and these stupid old legs – I just can't seem able to get myself turned over so as I can get up.' She attempted her grin.

Denis heaved her up and helped her sit on the doorstep. 'How long have you been there?' he asked. Her woolly cardigan was covered all over with bits of leaves, and earth.

'Lord, don't ask me. I done a bit of weeding, while I was down, and a bit of struggling, and a bit of cursing. But mostly I just been lying on my back watching that old seagull and wishing I was him. Always wanted to fly.' She patted the ugly bent legs. 'Daft, aren't I?

All those fairy stories we used to read together – remember them? Wish for this, wish for that...'

'Wait,' said Denis. 'I got something for you.' He ran quickly round to his own garden, pulled out the loose half-brick in the wall that hid the sugar-lump box, and was back before he had time to change his mind. 'This might help you to fly,' he said. 'One way or another.'

Next morning, Nellie was gone from her cottage, which didn't surprise Denis. From the school playground he gazed up at a wheeling seagull, and wondered if it was Nellie Maggs. He said as much to Mr Hornet, for he found that now, for the first time, he could talk about the happy day to Mr Hornet. Indeed, he was so happy, all the time, that he could talk to anyone, but the red-gold pearl was a secret between him and Mr Hornet – and soon, Nellie Maggs for he had a feeling that she wouldn't be so stupid as to try to hang on to that second happy day, as he and Mr Hornet had done.

'Could be,' said Mr Hornet. 'But I didn't find it made that sort of magic, did you?'

'No,' said Denis. 'In fact, it might not have *been* magic. It could all have happened anyway.'

ALISON MORGAN

Billy's Hand

I don't know what you've heard about Billy's hand. Everyone in the class has been so busy inventing, embroidering, twisting and magnifying what really happened that it's difficult to sort out the truth. Julia thinks, for instance, that it was a sort of collective waking nightmare brought on by the cheese in our sandwiches: I ask you! So that's what I've decided to do: tell you exactly what happened, exactly as I remember it. And I do remember it – after all, wasn't it me that Billy called for in that horrible moment? Miss Peters was there too, of course, but she's not going to give you an account of the events of that day, you can bet your boots on that. 'Hysteria,' she was muttering in the ambulance afterwards. 'An illusion induced by hysteria.' I don't know about that. I thought an illusion was something you saw that turned out to be not there at all, and you can't say that about Billy's hand, not really. But I'm jumping ahead. I mustn't do that. Back to the beginning.

Billy's hand. Doesn't it just sound like something from a horror movie? Could it be severed and dripping with blood? I'm sorry if this is a disappointment to anyone, but there are no severed heads, vampires, ghosts of the chain-rattling variety, headless horses or haunted graveyards, in this story; no matter what Sharon and Tracy may have told you. What you're going to hear may be more or less terrifying, I don't know, but I can say quite truthfully that I'd rather meet a couple of thirsty vampires any day than go through that again, perhaps because vampires, etc. have become quite cosy now that we see them on T.V. such a lot.

There's another reason why I should be the one to tell the story and that's because I'm Billy's cousin. I'm not only his cousin but I live next door to him and have done all my life. And there's something else: I'm probably the only person in the world, apart from his parents, who likes Billy. The truth is, he's awful. He's a bully, the worst sort of bully, nasty and thoughtful about his unkindness, as if he spends a great deal of time working out just the right torment for the person he's getting at. I know what they say about bullies, that they're all cowards at heart and that you only have to stick up for yourself and they'll run away. Well, our Billy's not like that. He's completely fearless. Or he was completely fearless, I should say. Before that school trip, there wasn't a person on earth he wouldn't have fought, and no one he would have feared to tease or terrify, not even kids with big brothers who threatened to have him beaten up after school, or those with dads who would report him to the Head as soon as look at him.

So why do I like him? Even love him a bit, perhaps. Well, firstly, as the vampires would say, blood is thicker than water. All my life he's been there like a big brother, and no amount of remembering the gouged-out eyes of my favourite dolls, or those dreadful frogs he used to put in my bed because they were my special terror, can change that. He could always run faster, climb higher, and shout louder than me, and so he gave me something to aim for, something to copy. Secondly, he became bored of bullying me by the time we were five. We went to school together (we've been in the same class all along) and there, spread out for his pleasure, were dozens and dozens of new victims, all fresh and ready with huge buckets of tears still waiting to be shed. I learned never to cry years ago. Thirdly, when we moved up into secondary school, he became a kind of protector, sheltering me from the lesser bullies of the class. 'Don't touch Kim Harrison,' they used to say, 'or that Billy'll get you, good and solid. She's his cousin or something.' And I was grateful for this protection, and did his homework for him most nights. I also made him promise to lay off all my best friends, but sometimes he forgot. He's not very bright, except at his bullying, you see, but at that he's fiendishly clever. One day, he cut off Shirley's thick, long plait of golden hair in the middle of a film we were watching in the school hall. It was a film about deserts, and suddenly Shirley shrieked and all the lights went on, and there was the cut-off plait under her chair, all lumpy and lifeless and horrid. I looked for Billy, but he was on the other side of the room. I'll never know how he moved so fast, nor what he did with the scissors. The Head never found out who had done it. There was no proof, though I bet he had his suspicions. Shirley cried and cried for hours all through dinner, even though it was sausages, which were her very best food of all. I screamed at Billy all the way home:

'You monster! How could you do it? I *told* you to leave Shirley alone. How could you? I'm not doing your homework for you for a month. Maybe I'll never ever do it again.'

'I forgot,' Billy said, smiling. 'That she was your friend, I mean. Doesn't matter, it'll grow. Teach her not to be so vain.'

'How come you're the one to punish everyone for their faults? Who gave you the right to teach people lessons? Brute, beast, I hate you!'

Billy didn't seem to be listening. 'If you don't do my homework,' he said, after some thought, 'I'll clobber you so's you'll stay clobbered, know what I mean?' He winked at me.

'Clobber away, go ahead and see if I care, you bullying gasbag!' I shouted and ran ahead. I'd managed to become a bit fearless myself over the years, and at that moment I was so furious about Shirley's hair, I'd have taken on a whole army of Billys.

'Run away, go on!' he yelled after me. 'Run away! GIRL! That's all you are, a silly girl. You only care about stupid Shirley's stupid old hair. You don't care about me.'

It wasn't until much later, in bed, that I began to wonder if Billy was jealous of Shirley. I hadn't been playing with him nearly so much lately. It was very peculiar.

Anyway, one day we went on a class outing to the Castle, a kind of history outing it was supposed to be. We went in a coach with Miss Peters (we call her Miss Piggy because she's plump and pink, with yellow hair bouncing round her shoulders, and a really turned-up nose) and Mr Melville, who's dry and long, like a stick with hair on top, and glasses. We took packed lunches from school and ate them in a field on the way. Most people were quite glad to be out for the afternoon, it didn't really matter what the reason was, but there were a few moaners, who kept saying things like:

'Boring old pile of rubbish.'

'Should've skived off.'

'Why can't they leave us here to play football and collect us on the way back?'

'Are there dungeons? I vote we lock Miss Piggy in with Old Melville!'

'I wouldn't mind so much, only they'll probably get us to write about it tomorrow. Do a project even.'

We drove a bit more after lunch, and when we first saw the Castle through the windows of the coach, everybody stopped talking. It was a very castle-like castle, square and high on top of a hill with tall, silent walls of thick, dark stone. I think Shirley was expecting a dainty turreted thing, like the Walt Disney cartoon castle in 'Cinderella' or 'The Sleeping Beauty'.

'Gosh,' she said to Miss Piggy, 'it's so square and grim-looking.'

Miss Piggy smiled: 'Well, dear, it *is* used as a prison still, you know.'

'Will we see them?' Shirley was anxious. 'The prisoners, I mean?'

'No, of course not. We shall be going on the guided tour, and they're in quite another part of the buildings.'

'We might hear their screams,' said Billy, and shrieked with laughter.

'William Harrison, behave yourself,' said Old Melville, 'or the screams you hear will be your own.'

'What'll you do, sir, lock him in the dungeons?'

'Chain him to the wall?'

'Hang, draw and quarter him?'

'Stick his head on a spike on the castle walls?'

'Shut-up!' I shouted, standing up in my seat. 'Don't be disgusting!' I sat down again next to Shirley.

'I think boys are revolting sometimes,' I said.

'It's not just the boys,' said Shirley. 'Lynn was the one who suggested chaining him to the wall.'

'Then girls are revolting, too. Everyone's horrible to Billy.'

'Billy's pretty horrible to them, though, isn't he?'

'Yes, I know. He is. Don't let's spoil the day by talking about him. I'm looking forward to it.'

'I'm not, really.' Shirley sighed. 'All these old things, they just don't seem real to me. I can't sort of take them seriously, know what I mean? It's as if it was a made-up story or something. I can't get worked up about things that happened donkey's years ago, not like you.'

After what happened to Billy, I asked myself over and over again whether I hadn't imagined the whole thing, but that was only to try and comfort myself, to convince myself that everything was in my own mind and nowhere else. But that's nonsense. It happened to everyone. To Billy most of all, of course, but something, something strange and something that I can't explain happened even to Miss Piggy and Old Melville.

When we got out of the coach, we went up some stone steps and waited for a while outside a small, wooden door that looked as if it hadn't been opened for centuries. But it did open, quite silently on well-oiled hinges and we went in.

The first room we saw was a courtroom, large and almost round, with high, light ceilings and a lot of heraldic shields up on the wall. The guide turned on a little silver tape-recorder and a voice spoke into the silence of us all sitting there, listening. The voice, floating up into the carvings over the windows, told us where to go next, and we followed the real guide into a small, round high room with tall walls, like a tower. Another tape-recorder (same voice) told us all about the things we could see all round us. Lots of us perked up a bit in this room, because it was full of horrible things in glass cases, like whips and cat-o-nine-tails and an iron, trap-like contraption called a scold's bridle, which was put over women's heads and was supposed to stop them talking too much.

'My mum could do with that,' someone said.

'What are those, sir, those kind of chains on the walls?'

'Neck chains,' said Mr Melville. 'Those big ones. And foot chains. Used to shackle people together on their way to the ships, to be deported to Australia.'

Near the wall was a large, wooden chair. Billy stood staring at it.

'What are you looking at that so carefully for?' I said.

'I'm trying to see how it works. It's jolly clever. You strap someone in, you see, and the more they struggle, the tighter the straps get. They used it for lunatics.'

'Charming, I'm sure,' I said and tried to laugh but the laughter wouldn't come. Everybody had turned quite quiet, even though the place was the opposite of gloomy. It should have been spooky, but it wasn't. It was neat, and brightly lit and quite cheerful in a peculiar kind of way. Even the dungeons, with thick stone walls and no light at all when the wooden doors were closed, were not too bad. We all took turns having the guide shut us in for a moment, and it wasn't very creepy, not with four or five others giggling and joking beside you. Miss Piggy came in with us, and Mr Melville went with the boys. Billy looked rather pale when he came out. He wasn't talking at all.

'I think it's a bit dull,' Shirley said.

'No, it must have been awful,' I replied, trying to picture it in detail and failing miserably. 'Think of that dark and the cold all the time, for months or years!'

'I know,' said Shirley. 'I know it was awful. But I can't *feel* it.' I said nothing because I couldn't really feel it either, and I was worried to think that my imagination was losing its power. It was like losing your sight, in a funny kind of way.

The next room we went into was also a courtroom, and the tape-recorded voice spoke hollowly of the trials that had taken place there. A kind of double metal bracelet was fixed to the wall of the prisoner's dock, and in the olden days, people found guilty had their hands locked into the iron bands and the letter 'M' for 'Malefactor' branded on the fleshy part of their hand below the thumb. The branding-iron was still there, too. I didn't stay to look at it more carefully. Suddenly, I wanted to leave, quickly. Just for a split second, I thought I had seen him: the judge. Dressed in purple, or red, or black, I couldn't quite see, and he was gone almost before my imagination had pictured him there, thin, skeleton-like under the carved oak canopy above him, with eyes that could burn you deep inside more thoroughly than that hideous branding-iron in the dock. My imagination had come back with a vengeance, I thought as I hurried out. But Shirley had seen him, too. She was white.

'Did you see him?'

'Who?' (I was playing for time.)

'A man. Thin and white-faced, like a skull. He was only there for a second. Then he was gone.'

'You must have imagined it.' I wasn't ready to admit anything at that stage.

Shirley cheered up. 'I'm sure I saw that man, but he can't have been real, can he, or he would have stayed put. Real people don't just vanish, do they?'

'No, of course they don't. Come on.'

Shirley came, looking quite comforted. I couldn't think why. Surely she would rather have seen a real person who stayed put? Hadn't she worked out yet that if what she saw wasn't real, it must have been something else?

The next room we went into (the last room we saw, as things turned out) is just a blur in my memory. I can't remember a word of the tape-recording, nothing about the room at all except – well. As soon as we were all crowded in, a shaft of sunlight came straight through the narrow window, and all of a sudden it was as if that

beam of brightness was the only thing in the world. I looked and looked at it, feeling as if I was drowning in the light. While this was happening, I could feel without knowing why, that everyone else was drawn into the light, too, staring, staring and powerless to move. I vaguely remember Miss Piggy's mouth hanging open. The light faded a little, and then came the noise, so much noise that I covered my ears. There was mist now outside the window, mist everywhere, although the sun was still shining, I'm sure of that. Through the mist, I saw them. We all saw them. We talked about it afterwards. There were thousands and thousands of them: faces, people, screaming throats and waving arms, all over the castle walls. It was hard to see what they were wearing, but it wasn't modern clothes. The people were watching for something, waiting for something. I knew I didn't want to see what it was they were waiting for. I took a deep breath and made a huge effort and turned my eyes away from the window. I saw Old Melville trembling, and blinking under his thick glasses. His mouth was opening and closing and his face was getting redder and redder. It was as if he were trying to speak and nothing would come.

'Are you all right, Mr Melville?' I said, because I honestly thought he was about to have a heart attack or something, and then two things happened. Mr Melville shrieked out: 'For God's sake, close your eyes, oh, close them, close them now. Don't look at it! Don't look at that hideous, that hideous . . . gibbet. Oh, save these children, save them from seeing it!' He fell on his knees, crying like a first-former. Miss Piggy rushed towards him, and everyone turned to see what the commotion was about. I glanced at the window. Nothing. No people. Silence. No gallows. I was just breathing a sigh of relief when I heard Billy. Hadn't he been with us all the time?

'Kim! Kim! Kim!' The scream went right through me, into my bones. I felt so cold, I didn't know how I would move. But I ran. Faster than I've ever run before, shouting:

'Billy, Billy, I'm coming!' I could hear footsteps behind me, and Miss Piggy calling 'Wait, Kim, wait for me!'

Billy was crouched on the floor of the courtroom, clutching his hand between his knees.

'My hand!' he moaned. 'Oh, Kim, look at my hand. I can't stand it, the pain, how will I ever stand it? He was crying and crying and rolling around to try and find a way to sit that wouldn't hurt so much.

'Let me see,' I said. 'Come on, Billy, let me see it.'

'No, no,' he sobbed, 'nobody must see it. Please, Kim, don't look!'

'Don't be such an idiot,' I said, 'how can we get it better if I don't see it?'

I reached down and took Billy's hand. Under the thumb, on the fleshy part of his left hand, clear as clear, the letter 'M' was branded into the flesh: red, sore, burning. I dropped his hand in terror and turned to run away and find help. I bumped straight into Miss Piggy.

'Billy's hand is branded!' I shrieked. 'It is! It is!'

'Shush, child, quiet. Sit down. Let me look at it.' She sat down on a bench, and put her coat round me and went to look at Billy.

'He's fainted,' she said. Mr Melville and the others had pushed their way into the room.

'Fetch an ambulance,' said Miss Piggy.

'He's been branded,' I cried. 'Look at his hand.'

'It's hurt, certainly,' said Miss Piggy. 'An ugly bruise and a bad cut, that's all, but it must be very painful. I wonder how he did that?'

'It's *not* a bruise,' I shouted. 'It's a mark. There's the branding-iron. Touch it. Go on. Touch it.' I wouldn't touch it. I wouldn't look at the judge's chair. I knew he would be there, the judge. Billy and I went in the ambulance with Miss Piggy. Mr Melville took the others back to school.

Billy's hand has a scar on it now. Just a coincidence, I suppose, that the scar happens to have the shape of an 'M'? That's the official story. They also said, the teachers and doctors, that the scar would fade. But it hasn't. Sometimes it's very pale and you can hardly see it, but sometimes it's very red and nasty. Billy rather enjoyed showing it off at first, but he never, not even to me, said a word about how he came to bear the mark in the first place.

ADÈLE GERAS

She Was Afraid of Upstairs

My cousin Tessie, that was. Bright as a button, she was, good as gold, neat as ninepence. And clever, too. Read anything she would time she were five. Papers, letters, library books, all manner of print. Delicate little thing, peaky, not pretty at all, but, even when she was a liddle un, she had a way of putting things into words that'd surprise you. 'Look at the sun a-setting, Ma,' she'd say. 'He's wrapping his hair all over his face.' Of the old postman, Jumper, on his red bike, she said he was bringing news from Otherwhere. And a bit of Demarara on a lettuce leaf – that was her favourite treat – a sugarleaf, she called it. 'But I haven't been good enough for a sugarleaf today,' she'd say. 'Have I, Ma?'

Good she mainly was, though, like I said, not a bit of harm in her.

But upstairs she would not go.

Been like that from a tiny baby, she had, just as soon as she could notice anything. When my Aunt Sarah would try to carry her up, she'd shriek and carry on, the way you'd think she was being taken to the slaughterhouse. At first they thought it was on account she didn't want to go to bed, maybe afraid of the dark, but that weren't it at all. For she'd settle to bed anywhere they put her, in the back kitchen, the broom closet under the stairs, in the lean-to with the copper, even in the coalshed, where my Uncle Fred once, in a temper, put her cradle. 'Let her lie there,' he said, 'if she won't sleep up in the bedroom, let her lie there.'

And lie there she did, calm and peaceable, all the livelong night, and not a chirp out of her.

My Aunt Sarah was fair put about with this awkward way of Tessie's, for they'd only the one downstairs room, and, evenings, you want the kids out of the way. One that won't go upstairs at night is a fair old problem. But, when Tessie was three, Uncle Fred and Aunt Sarah moved to Birmingham, where they had a back kitchen

and a little bit of garden, and in the garden my Uncle Fred built Tessie a tiny cabin, not much bigger than a packing-case it wasn't, by the back kitchen wall, and there she had her cot, and there she slept, come rain, come snow.

Would she go upstairs in the day?

Not if she could help it.

'Run up, Tessie, and fetch me my scissors – or a clean towel – or the hair brush – or the bottle of camomile,' Aunt Sarah might say, when Tessie was big enough to walk and to run errands. Right away, her lip would start to quiver and that frantic look would come in her eye. But my Aunt Sarah was not a one to trifle with. She'd lost the big battle, over where Tessie was to sleep. She wasn't going to have any nonsense in small ways. Upstairs that child would have to go, whether she liked it or not. And upstairs she went, with Aunt Sarah's eye on her, but you could hear, by the sound of her feet, that she was having to drag them, one after the other, they were so unwilling, it was like hauling rusty nails out of wood. And when she was upstairs, the timid tiptoeing, it was like some wild creature, a squirrel or a bird that has got in by mistake. She'd find the thing, whatever it was, that Aunt Sarah wanted, and then, my word, wouldn't she come dashing down again as if the Militia were after her, push the thing, whatever it might be, into her mum's hands, and then out into the garden to take in big gulps of the fresh air. Outside was where she liked best to be, she'd spend whole days in the garden, if Aunt Sarah let her. She had a little patch, where she grew lettuce and cress, Uncle Fred got the seeds for her, and then people used to give her bits of slips and flower-seeds, she had a real gift for getting things to grow. That garden was a pretty place, you couldn't see the ground for the greenstuff and flowers. Narcissus, bluebells, sweetpeas, marigolds.

Of course the neighbours used to come and shove their oar in. Neighbours always will. 'Have a child that won't go upstairs? I'd not allow it if she was mine,' said Mrs Oakley that lived over the way. 'It's fair daft if you ask me. *I'd* soon leather her out of it.' For in other people's houses Tessie was just the same – when she got old enough to be taken out to tea. Upstairs she would not go. Anything but that.

Of course they used to try and reason with her, when she was old enough to express herself.

'Why don't you go, Tessie? What's the matter with upstairs? There's nothing bad up there. Only the beds and the chests-of-drawers. What's wrong with that?'

And Aunt Sarah used to say, laughing, 'You're nearer to heaven up there.'

But no, Tessie'd say, 'It's bad, it's bad! Something bad is up there.' When she was very little she'd say, 'Darkwoods. *Darkwoods*,' and 'Grandfather Moon! I'm frightened, I'm frightened!' Funny thing that, because, of the old moon itself, a-sailing in the sky, she wasn't scared a bit, loved it dearly, and used to catch the silvery light in her hands, if she were out at night, and say it was like tinsel falling from the sky.

Aunt Sarah was worried what would happen when Tessie started school. Suppose the school had an upstairs classroom, then what? But Uncle Fred told her not to fuss herself, not to borrow trouble; very likely the child would have got over all her nonsense by the time she was of school age, as children mostly do.

A doctor got to hear of her notions, for Tessie had the diptheery, one time, quite bad, with a thing in her throat, and he had to come ever so many times.

'This isn't a proper place to have her,' he says, for her bed was in the kitchen – it was winter then, they couldn't expect the doctor to go out to Tessie's little cubbyhole in the garden. So Aunt Sarah began to cry and carry on, and told him how it was.

'I'll soon make an end of that nonsense,' says he, 'for now she's ill she won't notice where she is. And then, when she's better, she'll wake up and find herself upstairs, and her phobia will be gone.' That's what he called it, a phobia. So he took Tessie out of her cot and carried her upstairs. And, my word, didn't she create! Shruk! You'd a thought she was being skinned alive. Heads was poking out of windows all down the street. He had to bring her down again fast. 'Well, she's got a good strength in her, she's not going to die of the diptheery, at all events,' says he, but he was very put out, you could see that. Doctors don't like to be crossed. 'You've got a wilful one there, Missus,' says he, and off he goes, in high dudgeon. But he must have told another doctor about Tessie's wilfulness, for a week or so later, along comes a Doctor Trossick, a mind doctor, one of them pussycologists, who wants to ask Tessie all manner of questions. Does she remember this, does she remember that, when she was a baby, and *why* won't she go upstairs, can't she tell him the reason, and what's all this about Grandfather Moon and Darkwoods? Also, what about when her Ma and Pa go upstairs, isn't she scared for them too?

'No, it's not dangerous for them,' says Tessie. 'Only for me.'

'But *why* is it dangerous for you, child? What do you think is going to happen?'

'Something dreadful! The worst possible thing!'

Dr Trossick made a whole lot of notes, asked Tessie to do all manner of tests on a paper he'd brought, and then he tried to make her go upstairs, persuading her to stand on the bottom step for a minute, and then on the next one, and the one after. But by the fourth step she'd come to trembling and shaking so bad, with the tears running down, that he hadn't the heart to force her any further.

So things stood, when Tessie was six or thereabouts. And then one day the news came: the whole street where they lived was going to be pulled down. Redevelopment. Rehousing. All the little two-up, two-downs were to go, and everybody was to be shifted to high-rise blocks. Aunt Sarah, Uncle Fred, and Tessie were offered a flat on the sixteenth floor of a block that was already built.

Aunt Sarah was that upset. She loved her little house. And as for Tessie – 'It'll kill her for sure,' Aunt Sarah said.

At that, Uncle Fred got riled. He was a slow man, but obstinate. 'We can't arrange our whole life to suit a child,' he said. 'We've been offered a Council flat – very good, we'll take it. The kid will have to learn she can't have her own way always. Besides,' he said, 'there's lifts in them blocks. Maybe when she finds she can go up in a lift, she won't take on as much as if it was only stairs. And maybe the sixteenth floor won't seem so bad as the first or second. After all, *we'll* all be on one level – there's no stairs in a flat.'

Well, Aunt Sarah saw the sense in that. And the only thing she could think of was to take Tessie to one of the high-rise blocks and see what she made of it. Her cousin Ada, that's my Mum, had already moved into one of the tower blocks, so Aunt Sarah took Tessie out in her pushchair one afternoon and fetched her over to see us.

All was fine to start with, the kid was looking about her, interested and not too bothered, till the pushchair was wheeled into the lift and the doors closed.

'What's this?' says Tessie then.

'It's a lift,' says Aunt Sarah, 'and we're going to see your Auntie Ada and Winnie and Dorrie.'

Well, when the lift started going up, Aunt Sarah told us, Tessie went white as a dishclout, and time it got up to the tenth, that was where we lived, she was flat on the floor. Fainted. A real bad faint it was, she didn't come out of it for ever so long, and Aunt Sarah was in a terrible way over it.

'What have I done, what have I done to her,' she kept saying.

We all helped her get Tessie home again. But after that the kid was very poorly. Brain fever, they'd have called it in the old days, Mum said. Tossing and turning, hot as fire, and delirious with it, wailing and calling out about Darkwoods and Grandfather Moon. For a long time they was too worried about her to make any plans at all, but when she began to mend, Aunt Sarah says to Uncle Fred:

'*Now* what are we going to do?'

Well, he was very put out, natural, but he took his name off the Council list and began to look for another job, somewhere else, where they could live on ground level. And at last he found work in a little seaside town, Topness, about a hundred miles off. Got a house and all, so they was set to move.

They didn't want to shift before Tessie was middling better, but the Council was pushing and pestering them to get out of their house, because the whole street was coming down; the other side had gone already, there was just a big huge stretch of grey rubble, as far as you could see, and half the houses on this side was gone too.

'What's *happening*?' Tessie kept saying when she looked out of the window. 'What's happening to our world?'

She was very pitiful about it.

'Are they going to do that with my garden too?' she'd say. 'All my sweetpeas and marigolds?'

'Don't you worry, dearie,' says Aunt Sarah. 'You can have a pretty garden where we're going.'

'And I won't have to sleep upstairs?'

'No, no, Dad'll fix you a cubbyhole, same as he has here.'

So they packed up all their bits and sticks and they started off. Sam Whitelaw lent them his grocery van for the move, and he drove it too.

It was a long drive – over a hundred miles, and most of it through wild, bare country. Tessie liked it all right at first, she stared at the green fields and the sheep, she sat on Aunt Sarah's lap and looked out of the window, but after a few hours, when they were on the moor, she began to get very poorly, her head was as hot as fire, and her hands too. She didn't complain, but she began to whimper with pain and weakness, big tears rolled down, and Aunt Sarah was bothered to death about her.

'The child wasn't well enough to shift yet. She ought to be in a bed. What'll we do?'

'We're only halfway, if that,' says Mr Whitelaw. 'D'you want to stop somewhere, Missus?'

The worst of it was, there weren't any houses round there – not a building to be seen for miles and miles.

On they went, and now Tessie was throwing herself from side to side, delirious again, and crying fit to break her mother's heart.

At last, ahead of them – it was glimmery by then, after sunset of a wintry day – they saw a light, and came to a little old house, all by itself, set a piece back off the road against a wooded scarp of hill.

'Should we stop here and see if the folk will help us?' suggested Mr Whitelaw, and Aunt Sarah says, 'Oh, yes. Yes! Maybe they have a phone and can send for a doctor. Oh I'm worried to death,' she says. 'It was wicked to move the child so soon.'

The two men went and tapped at the door and somebody opened it. Uncle Fred explained about the sick child, and the owner of the house – an old, white-haired fellow, Aunt Sarah said he was – told them, 'I don't have a phone, look'ee, I live here all on my own. But you're kindly welcome to come in and put the poor little mawther in my bed.'

So they all carried Tessie in among them – by that time she was hardly sensible. My poor aunt gave a gasp when she stepped inside, for the house was really naught but a barn or shippen, with a floor of beaten earth and some farm stuff, tumbrils and carts and piles of turnips.

'Up here,' says the old man, and shows them a flight of stone steps by the wall.

Well, there was nothing for it; up they had to go.

Above was decent enough, though. The old fellow had two rooms, fitted up as bedroom and kitchen, with an iron cooking-stove, curtains at the windows, and a bed covered with old blankets, all felted-up. Tessie was almost too ill to notice where she'd got to. They put her on the bed, and the old man went to put on a kettle – Aunt Sarah thought the child should have a hot drink.

Uncle Fred and Mr Whitelaw said they'd drive on in the van and fetch a doctor, if the old man could tell them where to find one.

'Surely,' says he, 'there's a doctor in the village – Wootten-under-Edge, five miles along. Dr Hastie – he's a real good un, he'll come fast enough.'

'Where is this place?' says Uncle Fred. 'Where should we tell him to come?'

'He'll know where it is,' says the old man. 'Tell him Darkwoods Farm.'

Off they went, and the old man came back to where Aunt Sarah was trying to make poor Tessie comfortable. The child was tossing and fretting, whimpering and crying that she felt so ill, her head felt so bad!

'She'll take a cup of my tansy tea. That'll soothe her,' said the old man, and he went to his kitchen and brewed up some green drink in an old blue-and-white jug.

'Here, Missus,' said he, coming back. 'Try her with a little of this.'

A sip or two did seem to soothe poor Tessie, brung her to herself a bit, and for the first time she opened her eyes and took a look at the old man.

'Where is this place?' she asked. She was so weak, her voice was no more than a thread.

'Why, you're in my house,' said the old man. 'And very welcome you are, my dear!'

'And who are you?' she asked next.

'Why, lovey, I'm old Tom Moon the shepherd – old Grandfather Moon. I lay you never expected you'd be sleeping in the moon's house tonight!'

But at that, Tessie gave one screech, and fainted dead away.

Well, poor Aunt Sarah was that upset, with trying to bring Tessie round, but she tried to explain to Mr Moon about Tessie's trouble, and all her fears, and the cause of her sickness.

He listened, quiet and thinking, taking it all in.

Then he went and sat down by Tessie's bed, gripping hold of her hand.

She was just coming round by then, she looked at him with big eyes full of fright, as Aunt Sarah kneeled down by her other side.

'Now, my dearie,' said Mr Moon. 'You know I'm a shepherd, I never hurt a sheep or a lamb in my life. My job is to look after 'em, see? And I'm certainly not a-going to hurt *you*. So don't you be frit now – there's nothing to be frightened of. Not from old Grandfather Moon.'

But he could see that she was trembling all over.

'You've been scared all your life, haven't you, child?' said he gently, and she nodded, Yes.

He studied her then, very close, looked into her eyes, felt her head, and held her hands.

And he said, 'Now, my dearie, I'm not going to tell ye no lies. I've never told a lie yet – you can't be lying to sheep or lambs. Do ye believe that I'm your friend and wish you well?'

Again she gave a nod, even weaker.

He said, 'Then, Tessie my dear, I have to tell you that you're a-going to die. And *that*'s what's been scaring you all along. But you were wrong to be in such a fret over it, lovey, for there's *naught to be scared of*. There'll be no hurt, there'll be no pain, it be just like stepping through a door. And I should know,' he said, 'for I've seen

102

a many, many sheep and lambs taken off by weakness or the cold. It's no more than going to sleep in one life and waking up in another. Now do ye believe me, Tessie?'

Yes, she nodded, with just a hint of a smile, and she turned her eyes to Aunt Sarah, on the other side of the bed.

And with that, she took and died.

JOAN AIKEN

A Quiet Yippee

Looking down from Cousin Biddy's flat I couldn't see the stag-beetles however far from the window I leaned. All I could see were the tree tops and the heavy fan-out of leaves. The stag-beetles would be under the lowest branches, hovering.

Cousin Biddy hated them. She wouldn't even walk on the pavement. Instead she made her way down the exact centre of the street well clear of the greenery. Traffic was a lot less dangerous than stag-beetles, Biddy reckoned. This made me smile. Biddy was full of strange fads but her terror of beetles was very nearly the strangest.

'There are lots of stag-beetles down there,' I remarked. 'Swarms of them. Biddy's scared stiff of stag-beetles.'

'Scared of stag-beetles?' sniffed Mr Walsh. 'Nonsense.'

That was all he said. From the start Mr Walsh made it clear he didn't like kids – especially kids who came to spend all summer with Cousin Biddy. Mr Walsh was the most boring grown-up I'd ever met. He had the sort of face I forgot the instant I looked away from it. All I could recall was a greyish blob between his thin, crinkly hair and his stiff white collar even in August. Would he and Biddy really get married one day? They weren't a bit alike. It seemed to me Biddy's strangest fad of all was having Mr Walsh as a boyfriend.

'She shouldn't be long now,' I told him. 'She's been working late all this week. Biddy needs the overtime, she says.'

'I expect she does – a young cousin staying with her. I couldn't afford it. Can you see her coming?'

'The trees are in the way. You don't have to stop. I'll tell her you called.' Mr Walsh coughed.

'Thank you, Katherine. I'll wait if you don't mind. I've got something . . . something important to discuss with her.'

'I don't mind,' I said. 'Wait as long as you like.'

I did mind, though. Too much of Mr Walsh's company gave me pins-and-needles in the brain. Even worse, he stopped me reading. The hours and hours of reading I could do was what I like best about holidays with Cousin Biddy. Apart from Cousin Biddy herself, that is. Cousin Biddy was the least boring grown-up I'd ever met.

'Who's that?' asked Mr Walsh.

'That's Biddy!'

I heard the landing-door swing back and a clatter òn the stairs. As usual her voice came next – swooping like an air-raid siren. There was no chance to warn her.

'Yippeeeeeeeeeeeeeeeeee!'

Mr Walsh jerked upright in his chair as if he'd been struck by a thunderbolt.

'Er, Biddy....' I started to say.

She didn't hear me. Already she was working on her second yippee – a cross between a foghorn and seagull-screech.

'Yippeeeeeeeeeeeeeeeeee!'

This was her trumpet-of-a-dying-elephant version. Not that it mattered which version it was now.

'Yippeeeeeeeeeeeeeeeeee!' I replied.

'And about time too,' said Biddy. 'Didn't you hear me? You must be going deaf in your old age. Or more likely had your head in a book....'

Her voice trailed away. Mr Walsh stood up. His expression seemed to be drying on his face. His mouth moved up and down several times before he got the words out.

'Good evening, Bridget,' he said at last.

'What a surprise,' said Biddy, recovering. 'Hello, Henry. Have you been here long?'

'A little too long, Bridget, I'm afraid. I must leave straightaway.'

'Didn't you have something important to discuss?' I reminded him. 'That's what you said.'

Mr Walsh gave another polite cough.

'So I did. But we'll leave it for a future occasion, I think.'

'Are you sure?' asked Biddy. 'Let me —'

'I'm quite sure, thank you, Bridget. A future occasion.'

Stiffly, Mr Walsh bent to put on his cycle-clips.

'Goodbye Bridget,' he said. 'Goodbye, Katherine.'

He closed the door behind him. His footsteps echoed in the

hall-way. The door on the landing shut, too, far below, the front-door. I moved to the window and looked down. Somewhere beneath the leaves Mr Walsh was riding away.

'Poor Henry,' giggled Biddy. 'I must've sounded like an opera-singer gone barmy. Why on earth didn't you let me know he was here?'

'How could I? Anyway, didn't you see his bike as you came in?'

'I couldn't see a thing. I had the umbrella up.'

'The umbrella? In a heat-wave? Why?'

'To keep the stag-beetles off. In case they got caught in my hair. I'd rather look like a lunatic than have stag-beetles crawling on me. Just imagine, Kate – little cockhorneybug feet clip-clopping all over your face ... and in your ears ... or up your nose, even. Yuk!'

'Clip-clopping? Biddy, stag-beetles don't *clip-clop*. They haven't got horse-shoes on, you know.'

I had a sudden vision of a stampede of stag-beetles all trying to shoulder-charge their way up Biddy's nose. This thought was so daft it made me giggle. I found I couldn't even change the subject properly.

'Mr Walsh looked as if he'd *swallowed* a stag-beetle,' I spluttered.

'He looks like that most of the time,' Biddy said. 'Not that it matters. I'm no film-star myself.'

This was true. Dad once suggested Biddy got people laughing all the time so they couldn't get her ugliness into focus. Even now, when everything else in the room had a magic glint from the sunset, Biddy was left untouched. Her face was strong and friendly – but always reminded me of Dobbin the horse in one of my first picture-books.

'Biddy,' I asked. 'Will you really get married to Mr Walsh?'

'Why not? Prince Charles doesn't come round any more.'

'But Mr Walsh is so boring!'

'And I'm fat and forty and look like the back of a bus. Also it's the only offer I've ever had – or will be once he's made it.'

'That's not a good enough reason, is it? Shouldn't there be ... well, love?'

'Oh it could grow into love, Kate. There are different kinds. It's something you have to work at. Henry and me will do for each other.'

'But what about the yippees?'

'The what?'

107

'The yippees,' I said. 'You know – when you come in. He's not going to put up with that sort of thing, is he?'

'Not at first, maybe,' Biddy agreed. 'I'll have to quieten them down to begin with. They can come back to full strength later. When he's used to them. How about a cup of tea, Kate? I feel all fluttery after meeting Henry like that – and the best thing for a shock, as everyone knows, is hot, sweet tea!'

Tea was another of Biddy's fads. She drunk pints of it daily with about half a pound of sugar to soak it up. When I got back with the tray we both sat on the window-seat for a chat. I loved my chats with Biddy. They were part giggle and part gossip – about people she worked with in the factory, about what was happening in the world, about anything that took Biddy's fancy. Tonight, though, there was one subject for conversation only: that future occasion when Biddy and Mr Walsh would discuss 'something important'.

'He's going to propose to me,' Biddy declared. 'After all this time! Probably he'd have proposed by now if I hadn't made such a noise and put him off. Henry does love his peace-and-quiet! Never mind – it won't be long now before we're Mr and Mrs. Oh, I know you think he's a dry, old stick, Kate, but he's honest and hard-working and reliable. And maybe he'll liven up once we're wed.'

'Maybe you'll dull down,' I pointed out.

'Me?' said Biddy. 'Well, I do try to when I'm with him. But I can't help thinking I'm stuck the way I am – just plain scatty!'

Outside it was almost dark. From here to the horizon lamps blinked on as if bits of August had caught fire. I got up and crossed the room to the light-switch.

'Don't!' yelped Biddy.

'Don't what?'

'Don't put that light on. You'll have the room full of animals.'

'Animals?'

'You know, those cockhorneybugs – stag-beetles – whatever you call them. Shut the window first.'

'But it's hot, Biddy. We'll be sweltering in here.'

Biddy snorted.

'I'd rather swelter than be savaged by a stag-beetle.'

'Biddy —' I began.

A gentle thud against the curtain interrupted me.

'How can I see with the light off?'

From the window came a buzzing of wings.

'It's one of *them*,' hissed Biddy. 'It's an animal. *Do* something, Kate. Please! Agh! Aaagh! It brushed against me!'

'That was me, soppy. I'm looking for the newspaper.'

I folded the paper into a tight roll and listened for the next buzz. When it came I lashed out. The sound that followed was like a tiny model aircraft circling the room on the end of a string.

'You're just getting it angry,' Biddy protested.

'What else can I do? I'll get it in a minute. Hey! That was it!' The loud thwack was followed by a dead silence.

'Is it dead?' Biddy asked.

'Must be.'

'How do you know?'

'Well, what else could it be?'

'Stunned. Or just pretending – you know, sort of playing possum to trick us.'

'Biddy, insects aren't like that.'

Biddy laughed hollowly.

'That's what they'd like you to think.'

'Look, we've got to find it,' I said. 'If it's only stunned it'll be waking up in a minute. And if it's only pretending wouldn't you like to know where it is? Let me close the window first to stop any others getting in and *then* put the light on. Okay?'

Biddy shuddered and gave in. She crouched on the window-seat, her legs tucked under her, while I searched. I looked everywhere – the floor, the chairs, the tabletop and sideboard, even the mantelpiece. The insect had vanished. Yet there was a small brown mark on the newspaper. I'd been on target, definitely.

'I just don't get it,' I said. 'It must be here somewhere.'

'It's probably lying in wait,' groaned Biddy. 'As soon as I'm off my guard it'll ambush me.'

Gloomily, she reached for her seventh cup of tea that evening. Even as she sipped she was still scanning the room for the stag-beetle. Suddenly her eyes bulged, she choked, spat and hurled the cup across the room with a jungle-shriek.

'Whatever's the matter?' I exclaimed.

'The animal,' Biddy gibbered. 'It was there all the time – floating in my tea. I nearly swallowed it.'

She was right too. Amongst the broken china I found a small, sodden bluebottle.

'Hot, sweet tea,' I giggled. 'That's the best thing for a shock – you

certainly proved that! Especially if you've added a spoonful of insect!'

Even Biddy began to smile. By the time she remembered it was past my bedtime we were both laughing helplessly.

When eventually I got to sleep I dreamt of Biddy in a stiff, white collar and cycle-clips riding a stag-beetle to that future occasion she longed for so much. Next evening I decided to wait for Biddy down on the pavement beneath the trees. I was fed up with reading, for once, so I found a patch of honey-coloured light among the shadows and spread out my chalks. What should I draw?

'Hello, Katherine,' said Mr Walsh.

I looked in surprise.

'Hello, Mr Walsh.'

'Is your cousin expected home soon?'

'Any minute. There's no overtime tonight.'

'Ah . . . good.'

'Have you come for your important discussion?' I asked.

'What? Oh . . . er, possibly. Possibly. That's my business, I think.'

'Shall I draw you while we wait?'

'Draw me? On a public pavement?'

'With my chalks,' I explained. 'It won't take long. You won't have to get off your bike even.'

'Isn't there something else you can draw? One of the trees, say? That would be nice. Very artistic.'

'But I like drawing people. You wouldn't have to do anything.'

'Very well then – if you must,' Mr Walsh snapped. 'But don't expect me to sit still in this heat.'

He didn't either. He fidgeted with his clips, his tie, his watch and with something in the wicker-basket on the front of his bike. I didn't let it bother me. This time I was determined to remember Mr Walsh's face. I'd almost finished the portrait when he gave a gasp of astonishment.

'What on earth —'

I couldn't blame him for being surprised. Biddy's way of getting from the main road to her own front door was rather odd. She crept down the middle of the street huddled beneath her umbrella. She looked like a cat in a cartoon-film stalking a mouse.

'Is that . . . is that, Bridget?' asked Mr Walsh.

'That's Biddy,' I grinned.

'But why is she . . . what's she . . . how can she . . .?'

His voice trailed off. He was staring at me the same way he'd been goggling at Biddy. Even now it wasn't too late, though – or wouldn't have been if he hadn't looked back at my cousin. What she did next puzzled even me. She jerked the umbrella up and down furiously then swung round and round with wild lunges as if she were being attacked on all sides. She was squealing with panic. Finally, she hurled the umbrella high in the air. As soon as it had bounced back from the tree-branches and hit the ground she jumped on it with both feet.

'Got you – got you – got you!' she shrieked. 'That'll stop your clip-clop, clip-clop, clip-clop!'

This was enough for Mr Walsh. He was already pedalling away. His wobbling swerve round Biddy was so wide he almost mounted the pavement. Maybe he was terrified that if he fell off she might jump up and down on him. Biddy, though, didn't even look up as he passed her. She was too busy examining the wreckage of the umbrella. When she straightened up she was smiling. By the time she reached me she was laughing out loud.

'I am a clown,' she gurgled. 'Do you know what I just did? I thought I saw a stag-beetle so I started lashing out at it but I couldn't seem to shake it off – it seemed to be caught in the umbrella. In the end I was in such a state I threw the whole thing away then trampled on it just in case! Guess what it was all the time?'

'Not a stag-beetle?'

'No – it was the elastic bit with the bobble on the end. You know, the bit you stretch round the umbrella when it's folded up.'

She groped amongst the torn nylon and broken spokes to show me. The bobble-bit was the only part of the umbrella left intact.

'What an idiot!' Biddy crowed. 'Thank goodness Henry wasn't here. That would have been the end of our serious discussion, all right. What's the matter, Kate? Don't you think it's funny?'

'But he was here, Biddy. Look.'

She turned slowly. Where the avenue of trees ended, Mr Walsh perched on his bicycle with his right arm lifted. We watched him move off when the break in the traffic came, still wobbling but without a backward glance. Biddy had a look on her face I'd never seen before.

'Goodbye, Henry,' she said.

She sounded so faraway I think the biggest cockhorneybug in the world, complete with horse-shoes, could have tap-danced all round her and she wouldn't have noticed.

'Hey!' I exclaimed. 'We forgot our welcome-home yippee. Yippee!'

'Yippee,' whispered Biddy.

It was almost too soft to hear. The funny thing was I didn't know whether to laugh or cry either. I blinked and glanced down at the pavement. With my heel I began to scuff out the chalk-marks quickly.

CHRIS POWLING

The Shadow

It was on her very last day of school, when she was eighteen that Katie heard the remark about Eve. It was a day of 'Do you remember —' and 'Whatever happened to —' and someone had spoken Eve's name. She hardly took it in at first. When she did, she stood quite still and felt every nerve-end in her body creep against the skin as if it had suddenly come alive of its own accord. She fought against the memory but it came creeping back as inexorable, as dark as the night tide, pulled by that remark as the tide is pulled by the moon.

Summer: and she had just had her thirteenth birthday. Her brother, Rick, was fifteen, and he had been given his first stockwhip for Christmas. The long, hot Christmas holidays stretched ahead. There was plenty to do on the farm at this time of year, and neither of them had wanted any part of the holidays filled up with entertaining Eve, limp from her city suburb. 'Just a week,' said their mother. 'Her parents are such old friends, and she does go to your own boarding school. She can do whatever you do. You needn't alter your plans.' This was why, having no plans, they immediately made one to go to Whipcrack Falls. 'I've always wanted to go,' said Rick. 'Ever since old Charley told us what a wonderful hide-out it was for bush-rangers and how they never went there – not ever.'

'Funny,' said Katie, 'when you think how keen they always seemed to be to find nice secret places where they could hide the racehorses they stole.'

'And the gold and stuff they got from the stagecoaches,' said Rick. After a moment's silence he said, 'They must have been there at least once. How else would they know they didn't like it?'

'And why "Whipcrack"?' said Katie. 'Someone must have cracked a whip there – some time.'

'Charley said the bush-rangers called it that.'

'Why?' said Katie.

'That's what I'm going to find out. I'll have learnt to crack mine by then. O.K.?'

So they took Eve to Whipcrack Falls. She arrived as they knew she would, pale, tired and bendy about the knees. Her hair was long, fine and fair, her eyes were pale blue and her smile soft and compliant. She was helpful, willing, agreeable, even admiring, and not a complete fool. They could find nothing to dislike about her. It was necessary to ride to the Falls, and though she could not ride, she clung to the pommel on her quiet horse, went where they went and made no complaints. By the time they got to the place where they had to leave the horses they quite liked her.

It was the best kind of summer day – burning hot under the sun, cool in the shade and with a breeze that kept the air moving and brought whiffs of warm eucalyptus and baked earth and sometimes cow manure. The leaves on the eucalyptus showed sometimes silver, sometimes olive-green as they moved in the breeze, and strands of bark that hung from the creamy trunks rustled and swayed like beggars' rags. Birds and insects were busy, noisy and preoccupied. The track from where they had tied the horses led down into the deep gorge where the river ran. Here at the top they could hear the boom of the falls. And they looked down on the tops of trees and caught only a fugitive gleam of water far below. They walked in single file, Rick first with his whip over his shoulder, then Eve, then Katie with the pack of sandwiches on her back; and because it was almost midday each threw a short, black shadow on the track ahead. Katie saw Rick's shadow, steady and firm sliding over the dust and gravel, and Eve's, wavering, hesitating, splashing madly from side to side as she slipped and tripped and staggered along behind him, and she was filled with a small, unworthy feeling of satisfaction. Her own shadow, because of her shorter legs, was not quite as steady as Rick's but much, much steadier than Eve's.

At first they could see across the gorge to the trees on the far side and beyond the trees, to the golden undulations of the paddocks. Half way down they lost the breeze and it was very hot and still. The sound of the falls was louder and faint puffs of warm, moist air came up from below.

'Going to be hot at the bottom,' said Rick over his shoulder. 'We could swim.'

But it was not as hot at the bottom as they expected, for the steep northern side of the gorge blocked out the sun from long stretches of the river and the groves of she-oaks along its banks sheltered the surface on the southern side. Beneath the shadows the water tumbled and rushed over granite boulders that pushed up black and glittering from the river bed. Here and there a shower of spray caught a gleam of sunlight and sparkled like diamonds in the gloom. The track wound round a heap of rocks at the foot of the slope and came out on a patch of grass. Eve gave a small gasp, rushed to the river's edge, flung herself on her stomach and plunged her face into the water.

'Quite excited,' said Rick in mild surprise.

'She's hot and thirsty and she never said a word.' A lingering feeling of guilt made Katie unusually protective. She looked about her. 'Where are the falls then?'

'Further up. We've got a bit to go yet.'

They waited till Eve got up, her face wet and her chin dripping. She smiled vaguely. 'That was lovely. Thanks for waiting.'

'Come on. Lunch when we get to the falls.' He flicked the whip at a thistle head and let it trail along behind him over the grass.

They came out into a patch of sunlight at the edge of the grass and the track led round the slab side of a rock. Their three shadows splashed black against the rock as they passed.

On the other side the gorge widened and the river came to life, rushing and roaring through tumbled rocks, and sunlight streamed down into the open space. The track became more difficult as the rocks grew increasingly jumbled. But Rick climbed on, and the others followed. At last, clambering round one last barrier of rock, they saw the falls. The gorge ended in a horse shoe of high cliffs and from the top of the cliffs the river poured itself over, frothing white, to fall in one long streamer into a circular pool below. The pool was in shadow but the sun fell on the falling water and on half the cliff side. High up above the sky was blue and the tops of the trees tossed in the breeze. Where they stood there was no wind at all, but there were swallows flying over the pool, crossing and recrossing the rock walls, and wrens and finches darted in and out of shrubs that clung to the river's edge. Everywhere there was a sense of life and movement, and the cliffs, like ancient bastions, encircled and protected all.

'Now we can have lunch,' said Rick.

They were silent for a time, overpowered by the soaring cliffs, the turbulent water and the huge rocks that surrounded them. But food brings most things back to normal, and soon Katie heaved a sigh, leaned back on her arm and said, 'Except that it's a bit rough I can't see why the bush-rangers didn't want to come here.'

'Neither can I. And rough places make it harder to reach them anyway. It can't be that.' Rick did not sound particularly concerned. His lunch was occupying the greater part of his attention.

They watched the water tumbling into the pool and tried to calculate its depth. They saw where a small creek, creeping round the base of the cliffs on the south side, trickled its way through the rocks and came to join the river where the pool ran out downstream. They saw an eagle high above – a black spot in the blue sky – and they looked about to see if they could find its nest. They finished their sandwiches and lay back on the flat rock and gazed upward at the sky and the falling water. Eve's face grew pink and she said, 'I love it here. I'm so glad we came.' For the moment a bond of contentment and warmth drew them together.

Then Rick reached for his whip and climbed to his feet. 'You girls can stay here,' he said. 'I'm going to see what happens if I crack the whip.'

Eve sat up. 'Not too loud, please. It'll make a dreadful noise with the cliffs all round.' Her hair hung limp and tangled down her back. Katie saw her shiver before she lay back on the rock.

For a time they heard Rick's footsteps as he crunched his way over patches of gravel. Then they faded away and all they heard was the river plunging into the pool and the chattering of little birds in a patch of scrub just behind them. When Katie opened her eyes again she saw Rick standing on top of a high rock that overhung the pool not far from the cliff face. The whip hung from his hand and he was looking up at the wall of rock, and spray was falling on his face. He looked so remote, standing there, that just for a second she forgot he was her brother and took him to be part of his background – a statue on a plinth that was anchored deep in the centre of the earth. Then he turned to look at them, and saw her, and waved. 'Look,' she said to Eve. 'Look where he's got himself.'

Eve sat very still, looking at him. Then she said, 'Well, his cracking won't bother us from there.' But she did not lie back again.

They saw Rick move his legs apart and stand firm. They saw him lift the whip and swing it a few times slowly round his head. And then he began to crack it. The first few cracks were neither clean nor loud. But he went on and each time the crack became louder and clearer. The swing became, not faster, but more purposeful, and with each crack they could see his body bend again for the next. Occasionally he stopped and looked about, and each time he let the echo fade before he swung the whip again. On and on he went, and after a time he no longer paused between the cracks, but swung and cracked, swung and cracked, on and on, and now the sound rang out, echoing round the cliffs and filling the gorge with a kind of throbbing. Then, as the cracks came faster, and the figure on the rock became somehow possessed, swaying in time with the circling whip, the girls stood up. Eve put her hands over her ears, for the sound was all round them, filling the empty spaces, quivering through them, pinning them to the ground. Then, quite suddenly, it stopped. They saw the figure sag, saw the whip fall to its side, and saw Rick sink down on to the rock.

But the sound still held the air, and it was as if everything else had stopped. There was not the slightest breeze, no bird chattered, the falling water looked frozen, static, the sun itself was drained of light. The sound held everything. The air seemed poised, waiting. The cliffs looked blacker than ever, and were they leaning inward now, throwing a deeper shadow over the figure on the rock? What moved? Eve screamed, and clapped both hands over her mouth. The blackness of the cliffs appeared to move, to detach itself from the walls of rock and flow out over the pool. Katie could no longer see Rick, and as she stood, incapable of movement, it seemed to her that the blackness transformed itself into the shape of a bird, and the black, outstretched wings were all over them. She thought the great beak opened, and from it came a cry that seemed to echo from every quarter of the gorge – harsh, ear-splitting and appalling. The shriek that Eve gave before she fell down was one that Katie tried ever afterwards to forget. Then the darkness lifted, the last echo of sound died away and the interrupted day went on.

Little by little light, sound and movement returned. There was no black bird anywhere. Katie was still standing. The sound still rang in her ear. She looked down at Eve, and saw that she had raised herself on the palms of her hands and was looking about with wide, unblinking eyes. Her face was paler than ever and there was no expression in it of any kind. But she seemed all right. Katie looked up at the rock then, and saw that Rick was climbing to his feet. He took a few steps, bent down and picked up the whip. He turned again and she saw him lift his head to look long and hard at the cliffs.

They stood as they had always stood, towering, solid, supporting the table-lands above, releasing the river into the pool below. She saw his shoulders hunch briefly and then he jumped down out of sight and in a few minutes appeared between two lumps of granite and came to them.

'What a row,' he said. 'Grand, wasn't it? But it made me giddy. Did you see me fall over?' He was perfectly normal.

'Didn't you see —' said Katie, and stopped. The day was as it had been, birds, water, spray and the sun beginning to sink into afternoon. She shook her head. 'Nothing,' she said. 'I just had a funny feeling.'

Eve was on her feet now, too. Her eyes were still wide and vaguely searching. But she said, 'I had a funny feeling too. Something hurt me, but it's gone now. All that noise, and the echo like a drum beating. Can we go home now?' It was the first time she had ever asked for anything.

'Katie?' Rick looked at her.

'Let's go,' said Katie and picked up the empty sandwich pack.

They went back as they had come, Rick leading, Eve in the middle and Katie last. They climbed the whole way in silence. As they rose up they came out into the breeze and the sun again. Once Rick stopped, and they all stopped and turned. The falls were out of sight, but the river lay far below, deep in shadow now, already submerged in the first tides of night. They moved on – up into the bright afternoon. Their shadows lay behind them, longer, thinner and less opaque. It wasn't until they were near the top that Katie with her eyes on the ground in front of her halted in her stride, blinked and looked again. Then she looked up – at the sunny sky and the waving branches of the trees. She looked down again, and her eyes did not leave the track until they reached the top. She waited until they had got Eve on to her horse before approaching Rick, who was on the far side of his own horse, tightening the girth.

'Rick —'

'What's the matter?'

'Eve. She hasn't got a shadow any more.' If she had not been able to turn him and make him look he would never have accepted it as a serious statement. But there was Eve on her horse, and the shadow of the horse was plain on the ground. Where Eve's shadow should have been was bright sunlight. Even so, he said, 'Funny, but there'll be some kind of explanation. Don't worry. Let's get on home.'

The next few days passed quietly. Sometimes Rick was off with the men, working, but often the three of them were together. The weather remained fine and hot. There was ample opportunity to observe Eve unnoticed. After a couple of days Rick said to Katie, 'You're right. She never has a shadow now. It's gone.'

Katie had been observant, too, and now they were alone and together she said what she had been trying not to say until now. It came out in a high, strained voice. 'Rick, she still has a shadow, but it's not – it's not stuck to her. It's all over the place.'

They found the idea so horrible that there was a silence between them. After a time Rick said, 'I'm sure you must be wrong. But I'll look. I'll see if I can find it, too.'

There seemed nothing especially wrong with Eve. If she was quiet she had always been quiet. If they sometimes caught a slightly worried expression on her face, an absent look in her eyes it could have been caused by any one of a number of ordinary things. She was in unfamiliar surroundings, after all. It could have been their own imagination.

Then the weather broke and storm clouds built up, and for several days they did not see the sun at all. The change in Eve was notice-able. She lost that absent gaze. She laughed and talked, and where she had been listless before, she became active and alert. And their mother said her holiday was doing her a lot of good. The storms passed, the sky cleared, and the sun came out again, sucking up the moisture in the ground, putting a crust on the earth and making the garden flowers hang limp. And Eve relapsed into her previous lassitude, her eyes became vacant again and her smooth white forehead corrugated with bewilderment.

'She's not quite as well as she was,' said their mother.

After a week Rick took Katie walking behind the machinery sheds. 'You're right,' he said. 'It's there, but it's sometimes with you and sometimes with me, and sometimes just anywhere. It's never with her. And it's making her sick. Do you know what I think?'

Katie drew a deep, thankful breath and said, 'Yes?'

'We've got to take her back to the falls again. Maybe I should take the whip, too.'

'Rick, no!'

But they went. Two days later when the oportunity came, they went again. They tried to make it appear a happy holiday picnic, but Eve did not want to come and they had to use subtle threats, like Mum saying perhaps she should take her to the doctor, or keep her in bed. She had never been difficult to persuade, and she came, but she no longer smiled. Rick took his whip, and Katie prayed he would not use it. Except that the air was stiller and more humid it was a day very like the last. They tied the horses where they had tied them before and they walked down the track as they had before – with one difference. Eve walked behind, for Katie did not wish to look at the place where her shadow should have been. And they came in silence to the place where they had picnicked before. The air was oppressive and felt stale on their sweaty faces. Not a leaf twitched and the birds were very quiet. Today no eagle floated above the cliffs. The storm came up as they finished their lunch. They took what shelter they could against the overhanging rock as the first grumblings of the storm rolled up the gorge.

The cracks of thunder grew louder and became more frequent, echoing against the cliffs and bouncing back so that in the end the echoes merged with the next crack, making one continuous roar punctuated by loud explosions. Under the cliffs the light had gone and the pool was dark except when the flashes of lightning

illuminated all with an unearthly light as if a flame from Hell had shot up to pierce the black cliff walls. Then one flash came, aiming direct at the tallest of the trees that lined the top of the gorge. They saw the tree split, burst into flame and topple over the rim and down the slope. At the same time there came a clap of thunder louder than any before.

'Crack the whip now!' Eve suddenly shouted.

Rick, as if he had been waiting for just this, sprang out from the shelter of the rock. He swung the whip again and again. And once more came the sense of throbbing, even at the height of the storm. And, as if drawn by the sound, a blackness came from the foot of the cliffs, rose up and spread over them like outstretched wings, and the sound they heard through and above the thunder was the cry of a bird of prey.

Rick jumped back under the rock. Pressed together as they now were, he and Katie felt Eve go rigid, shiver and then draw a long, shuddering breath. They thought she was going to fall, but she did not. Instead, she shook them off and stepped forward.

'This is what we came for,' she said. Her voice rang with confidence and force. But there was another note in it, too, and it was this that gripped the others in the stomach and wrenched at their nerves. It held a strange, high coldness that sounded, in this place and at this time, scarcely human.

The rain came flooding down, roaring into the pool, bouncing off all the rocks, pouring into the river, and when it was over, Rick said, 'We'd better go home', and led the way back up the hill. The sun came out before they had gone far, shining on the dripping leaves, steaming on the muddied track. And Katie's eyes were drawn to Eve against her will. The shadow was there again, following obediently where she trod. They stopped to get their breath, for Rick had led them at a smart pace. Something forced them all to turn and look back. But there was no longer anything to see. From out of the gorge rose a thick, white mist, billowing up the slopes, coiling round the trees, blotting out sound and sight. They looked into a void. Before they turned again Katie saw Eve's face, and thought for a moment it was the face of a stranger. The blue eyes had narrowed, the wide, soft lips, so often gently smiling, were pressed thinly together and all the muscles were tight against the skin. The expression was closed and secret, as if it held in a power that threatened to burst out – a power that was not benevolent. Then she was looking at the soft, pale hair that fell down Eve's back, and they were moving on.

Near the top they had to walk round the edge of a steep rock at a place where the slope was sheer. There were no handholds on the face of the rock and the drop below was straight down almost to the river. But the track was wide enough and they had thought so little of it, climbing up this time, that when Katie's shoelace came untied she stopped without thinking and leaned down to tie it up. Eve stopped too, and perhaps she tripped as she turned, or perhaps the height made her suddenly giddy, for she lurched against Katie and would have sent her, unbalanced as she was, over the edge if Rick had not grabbed her quickly and pulled her back.

'Oh,' said Eve. 'Oh, Katie, I'm dreadfully sorry.' But as they continued on again Katie heard her give an odd little giggle and she was glad she could not see her face.

They reached the horses and, as usual, Rick and Katie first helped Eve to mount. For the first time the old horse refused to stand, but circled and snorted and laid its old ears back. They thought Eve would be frightened, but when they got her up she broke a switch from the nearest tree and began to lash his ribs. 'I'll show him,' she said through clenched teeth.

They got home more quickly than usual and for once Rick took all the horses and told Katie and Eve to go and change. He walked away with the horses before anything could be said.

By the time dinner was over that evening any tension there may have been had slipped away, and when they played Scrabble as they usually did, Eve's eyes were just as big and round and slightly helpless as they always were, her expression as gentle and her smile as frequent. A couple of times Katie caught Rick watching her, but she lost as amiably as usual. Later, when Katie climbed into her bed she was almost able to believe nothing unusual had happened except in her own over-excited imagination.

She must have fallen asleep at once, for she had the feeling she had been sleeping for hours when she woke up again. She thought it was a nightmare that had woken her for her nerves were tingling and somewhere there was fear. But everything was quiet and the only noises were the usual noises of the house and the fainter noises of livestock in the paddocks. Besides, it could not be very late, for she saw that the hall light still shone through her open door. She closed her eyes and tried to sink back again to sleep. But her nerves remained tight and the creeping fear that had woken her came up from her stomach and began to set her heart pounding. Sleep was gone until she located the source of the fear. She lay still while she came back to full wakefulness. She pulled the sheet slowly back from her face so that she could see through the door into the passage. There was a figure standing in the doorway, the light behind sending a long shadow to the foot of the bed. It was Eve. She was standing motionless and Katie knew she was watching her. In her sleep she had already felt that boring look. Suddenly she was very cold. Then Eve giggled quietly. The whole room was suddenly full of the figure in the doorway. It flowed across the ceiling, black, outspread, like wings, and dropped down over the bed.

Then at the end of the passage someone switched the light out. As if released, Katie sat bolt upright. 'What are you doing, Eve?' she said loudly.

The voice that answered her was perfectly normal – quite ordinary. 'I just came to say goodnight. I'm sorry if I disturbed you. Goodnight, Katie.' Then she heard the door shut, and when she switched on the light by the bed there was no one there. The next day they spent inside. Rick had work to do, he said. And Katie stunned her family by mending her clothes all day. Eve, cooperative as ever, sat and read, or helped in the kitchen. In the two remaining days of Eve's visit the weather changed. The sun disappeared behind low clouds and it began to rain. It rained solidly for a week so that they could not go outside. Long before the week was over Eve had gone back to her suburb.

Eve spent no more holidays with them. For a few weeks after her visit their parents talked of her occasionally. But between Rick and Katie a great silence fell. Then in May when they were at home again their mother received a letter from Eve's mother. She picked it up with a small cry of pleasure and tore it open. It was only when Katie had finished reading the long and absorbing letter from her own best friend that she noticed her mother still had the letter in her hand. She had ceased to read it and she was standing very still.

'Mum?' said Katie sharply.

Her mother turned, seemed to look at the space just above Katie's head and walked slowly away with the letter in her hand.

It was after this that she and Rick became aware of the silences that now fell between their parents. At last Rick said, 'It's about Eve. We've got to know what it is.'

When they pressed him their father said bluntly, 'Someone thought Eve tried to kill a child.' Katie felt a frozen weight in her stomach. It was not caused by surprise. On the contrary, it was there because she found that she was not surprised.

'An accident, of course,' said their mother quickly. 'She simply tripped on the kerb and fell against the little boy. Her mother's sure she couldn't have seen the car coming.'

'Did she – was the little boy —' Katie's voice was unexpectedly shrill.

'The car swerved. It was all right,' said their father. 'Unfortunately someone saw it and got the impression —'

'Was it a fine day?' said Rick suddenly.

Their parents were bewildered by the question. It was difficult to find out if the sun had been shining, but in the end they managed to discover that it had been a warm, humid morning, culminating, just after the event, in a sharp thunderstorm.

'Stormy weather makes people jumpy,' said their mother.

But they knew the storm had nothing to do with it. When the police came (for the woman who saw the incident had insisted on summoning them, holding on to Eve's arm until they arrived) Eve had been so upset and remorseful and so distressed for the child's sake that at last everyone had believed it had been no more than an accident narrowly averted. Even the woman who had seen it changed her mind and to make amends had accompanied her home to reassure her parents. Only the tone of the letter revealed that they had not been entirely reassured.

'You see,' said Rick afterwards, 'the sun was out when she did it. By the time the police had come it had clouded over.'

'No shadow,' said Katie, and Rick nodded.

After this they wondered if they should tell what they knew. 'But what do we know?' said Rick.

'There's one thing I know,' said Katie. 'You can crack your whip at the Falls till Doomsday. Nothing'll happen now.'

They never spoke of it again, but they knew that whatever haunted the Falls had found its home at last. The shadow of – whatever malevolent creature it had been was now Eve's shadow. And the shadow was stronger than Eve.

From that time until the day, five years later, when Katie heard the remark about Eve they, too, were haunted – by the thought that someone should be warned. But why? And of what?

'Poor old Eve,' the girl had said. 'She's had some kind of a breakdown. She's in an institution.' Then the voice had dropped. 'They say she'll never come out.'

Katie told Rick at once, and because their parents had kept silence they, too, never spoke of the weight that had slipped from their shoulders.

JOAN PHIPSON

The Whistling Boy

It came to a head the day that Bonzo watered the garden.

'I was only trying to help,' he said.

The others, gathered near the park gate, were laughing, as they had been for some minutes. Several were even draped over the low railing around the shrubbery, weak with the strain.

'How long did you say it took?' said Tom Jex, his great friend.

'Well it's only a small garden,' said Bonzo.

'I know.' Tom had quite often been in the garden even though, if Bonzo's grandmother were there, they would be driven out pretty quickly. It was more a yard than a garden, very tiny, with an old wash-house along one side, and tall walls. The bit that could be called a garden was a strip of earth along one side. It was full of flowers – or had been.

'It only took two watering cans,' said Bonzo.

'And how much weed killer did you put in?'

Bonzo's large, pink face took on a slightly redder shade. 'Only what was left in the packet,' he said.

'But you told me you'd just opened a new one.'

'Well, I mean,' said Bonzo, 'I only used what was left when I filled the second can.'

There was a splutter from the railings.

'So you used it all?'

'Well, I suppose so.'

'And how long,' said Tom carefully, 'did it take to show?'

'Oh I don't know.' Bonzo showed signs of wanting to change the subject. He gave the railings a shake to the great danger of the draped figures.

'I mean,' Tom insisted, 'did the flowers begin to droop straight away?'

'Of course not!' Bonzo was indignant. He had been thoroughly misunderstood. 'They didn't go brown until teatime!'

There was a dull thud as two figures, like shot rooks, fell from the railing and lay on the grass in the dusk, wheezing and rattling as they fought for breath.

'What did it look like next morning?' said Tom.

'Oh well, that's different, of course.' Bonzo, having made his point that the disaster hadn't come about as quickly as everybody believed, was quite prepared to describe the dramatic outcome once again. 'All their petals had dropped off and they'd all bent over. Most of them lay quite flat.' He thought for a moment. Then he said, frowning as he tried to imagine it, 'I should think that if you got a flame-thrower and gave them a good blast they would look a bit like that. You know, burnt.'

Tom doubled up and joined the others on the grass. They kicked and heaved and wheezed, but after a time the pain was not so great and they sat up.

'What about your Mum?' said one of the others.

'Oh she wasn't so bad. She laughed a bit.' Bonzo's plump face was smiling benignly. He was pleased to have amused so many people. But then he frowned as though he had felt a twinge. 'It's my Granny that's the trouble.'

Tom knew very well what he meant. Bonzo's mother was very much like Bonzo himself, tall and plump and rather stately, never greatly troubled by anything. His father had died long before Bonzo could remember, and his grandmother had moved in. She was much smaller than her daughter but bullied her. She had hair of iron grey clamped close to her head like a helmet, steel-rimmed glasses, a downturned mouth and a voice that clattered like a box full of cutlery.

'She tried to catch me,' he said, 'but I ran out of the house and had dinner with my Mum up town.'

Bonzo's mother worked in a shop on the Market Place and sometimes, in the holidays, he would go to a café with her for lunch. They both knew that the house was too uncomfortable for him with only his grandmother there.

It was getting dark. Across the park, shadows were thickening beneath the trees as though the darkness was growing upwards to join the branches to the ground. A massive silence had descended over the whole town, bringing with it a kind of sadness. Tom looked at Bonzo. There was just enough light on his face to show that the sadness had crept into him and, with a kind of chill surprise, Tom felt what it was like to be Bonzo. In a moment he would put his friends behind him and wander away to the other side of the park to the tiny house which his steely grandmother had made into a cold prison.

He wished he could ask him to his own house; that would cheer him up. But it was too late. Instead, he said, 'Tell you what.'

Bonzo looked up. 'What?'

'I'll walk home with you.'

'That's not much of a tell-you-what.'

They laughed and were still in a good mood when they reached Bonzo's house. It was in a jumble of narrow streets crowded close to the park but hidden from it by the tall trees. At the front the house was darkness, but downstairs the curtains were slightly parted and Tom could see the pale glimmer of the plaster figure that stood on a little pedestal in the window. It was a barefoot boy standing with his hands in the pockets of his ragged trousers and with a floppy hat pushed to the back of his head.

'He's always happy, anyway,' said Tom, feeling the gloom begin to descend once more on Bonzo.

'Do you reckon?'

'Well he never stops whistling.'

The boy had his head thrown back as he blew, and he obviously had no care in the world.

'I can't understand it,' said Bonzo. There was no need for him to say any more; they both knew the whistling boy was one of his grandmother's possessions, and she had nothing to do with happiness.

As Bonzo pushed open the front door, Tom held the knocker to prevent it rattling. They could hear voices from the room at the back, but with luck Bonzo would be able to get to bed without once more having to suffer his grandmother's wrath.

'See you tomorrow,' said Tom.

'If I survive.'

The door closed softly.

Next afternoon they were playing cricket in the park, but not very well. Bonzo, mainly because of his plumpness, fancied himself as a slow bowler, but he seemed to think that the only skill a slow bowler had to have was slowness, and that the slower he was the more batsmen he would get out. The result was he strolled up to the wicket and sent up gentle lobs that did not always get to the far end. Batsmen loved him, but fielders got tired running for the boundary, and the game soon petered out.

'You want to try sending it down a bit faster, Bonzo,' said one of his team.

'You can't get spin if you bowl fast,' he said.

'What spin?'

'The way I do it.'

'That ball wasn't spinning. It floated.'

'Like a balloon,' said someone.

'You could read the maker's name on it,' said someone else.

'And count the stitches.'

Bonzo looked at them loftily. 'Very funny,' he said.

'Watch out,' said Tom, trying to protect him, 'you'll make him mad.'

'He's gone red already.'

'He'll go green in a minute.'

'Like the Hulk.'

'Bonzo the Hulk.'

'Let's see your shirt split, Bonzo.'

'His trousers are tight enough already.'

It was getting worse. Tom broke in again. 'He could beat any of you lot,' he said. There were no challengers. 'Any two of you.'

Those who had been taunting Bonzo, now lay on the grass as though the subject held no interest.

'Come on,' said Tom to him. 'They're not worth bothering with.'

They wandered away together and Bonzo, who had enjoyed his cricket in spite of everything, became silent. Tom looked at him. Bonzo was having a bad time. He was in trouble at home, and now his friends were making fun of him.

'Come and have tea at our house,' he said suddenly.

Bonzo brightened but it was not because of the invitation. 'No,' he said. 'You come round mine.' He saw Tom's surprise, and added quickly, 'It's all right, my Gran's gone out.'

The little house was quiet except for the hum of the canning factory at the end of the street. They went up to Bonzo's bedroom. It was very neat and Bonzo was apologetic. 'I used to have a battle scene on that chest of drawers,' he said. 'Tanks and aeroplanes. But she came and swept them all away.'

'Not your Mum.'

'No. She said I could do it, but Gran came and did it when there was nobody at home. There was a row about it and my Mum said I could put 'em back, but I thought I'd better not.'

'You're afraid of her.' Tom could not resist it. 'You're frit.'

'I ain't.'

There was a long pause and then Tom said something that soon he was to be sorry for. 'Prove it.'

Bonzo was no coward. 'All right,' he said.

Tom knew it meant more trouble, and Bonzo had more than enough. 'I didn't mean it,' he said, and tried to restrain him, but it was too late. Bonzo had picked up something from the table beside his bed and was heading out of the room. All Tom could do was follow.

They clattered downstairs and into the front room. Bonzo went straight to the figure of the whistling boy.

'She's always polishing him,' he said. He had a strange look on his face. It was almost savage. Something had come to the surface from beneath all the layers of his good nature, and Tom could do nothing about it. 'She really treasures this.' Bonzo was lifting the statue of the whistling boy from its pedestal.

'Careful.' Tom was alarmed. 'You'll break it.'

'So what.' It was a different Bonzo. His plump face was flushed and his dark eyes were feverish and hard. 'She bust my aeroplanes,

I'll bust her blasted boy.' He thumped the figure on the carpet, but breaking it was not his intention. He still had in his hand the object he had picked up in his bedroom. It was a pencil box and he opened it to spill out its contents.

'I've always wanted to do this.' He picked up a felt pen. It was green, and he began stabbing it at the shining glaze of the boy's face. 'Measles,' he said. 'Worse. Bubonic plague.'

The spots multiplied, spreading to the arms and even the legs beneath the ragged edges of the trousers.

'Looks serious,' said Tom.

'Fatal.'

Bonzo put the green pen aside and picked up a brown one. He began drawing in a heavy moustache. Tom laughed, but his heart was not in it. It was not that he minded Bonzo defying his grandmother, it was more that there was something about the whistling boy he liked. He wore rags but didn't care. He had his bare feet thrust into grass and, as he gazed out into the world, he whistled.

'He doesn't look a bad old boy,' he said as the rather girlish rosebud lips disappeared beneath Bonzo's pen. 'I shouldn't think he'd mind dressing up.'

'You reckon?' Bonzo looked up. The burst of activity had driven away some of his feverishness. 'I always thought him and me could be mates.' He was silent for a moment and then said, 'If it wasn't for her.' He stood up and lifted the plaster figure. 'Come on then, Whistler, let's see what you look like on your platform.'

The whistling boy was quite large and heavy, so they lifted him together. He had the face of a spotty, leering old man and they began to laugh.

'He looks a lot better like that,' said Bonzo. 'And I know some other people who could be improved.'

'So do I,' said Tom.

They were kneeling on the carpet drawing moustaches on each other when a shadow fell across them. They looked up. For a moment Tom thought the whistling boy was toppling from his pedestal, but then a rap on the glass drew his eyes beyond the boy to the window. The light was behind her, but there was no mistaking her shape or the glint of steel in her helmet of hair.

The window shook to a hailstorm of raps as her fury could not be contained. Then she vanished. They heard her foot scrape on the step and a moment later her tread in the hallway.

132

The door swung back and she stood there, slightly bent, her head thrust forward. There was a mesh of fine wrinkles over her grey skin and her mouth was pulled fiercely down at the corners. Her eyes glittered.

'Ha, my lad!' Her voice was sharp and full of triumph. 'You don't get away with it this time!'

'I didn't damn well get away with it last time.' The words were no more than a mutter, but Bonzo's daring made Tom go cold. He saw the old woman's lips vanish in a bunch of tight wrinkles, and then her voice came again in a kind of subdued shriek.

'Mary!' The large shape of Bonzo's mother appeared behind her. 'Mary, did you hear what that boy said to me!'

'No, Mother.'

'Filthy words, Mary! Filthy words!'

She advanced and a faint smell of lavender came with her like the sweet odour of a venomous animal.

Tom began to move backwards but Bonzo, in front of him, held his ground. Her head weaved slightly as though she was looking for a place to strike. Then she straightened.

'Come here, Mary.' Her voice was less loud, but certain of victory. Her eyes remained fixed on Bonzo and, as his mother came forward, Tom risked a glance at the statue. The whistling boy's face was turned away from the old woman and she had not yet seen his decorations.

The voice grated again. 'I want you to go to my purse in the sideboard drawer, Mary, and count the money.'

The large, round face of Bonzo's mother was astonished. 'Mother, what are you saying?'

'I'm saying, Mary, that your son cannot be trusted. He knows he's not supposed to come into this room. He knows because I have told him over and over again that everything I treasure is kept in here. And yet he defies me and brings his thieving little friends into the house, and when I catch them red-handed he flings filthy words in my face!'

'Mother!'

The old woman had drawn herself rigidly straight. She clutched her handbag to her stomach. 'Just look at them,' she said. 'There's guilt written all over their faces.'

It was her first mistake, for Bonzo's mother, coming further into the room, at last saw them clearly. Her expression changed.

'What on earth have you been doing?' she said. She seemed to find it difficult not to laugh.

'Nothing,' said Bonzo innocently. He glanced at Tom. 'Have we?'

But now they saw each other again, heavily spotted and with drooping moustaches.

'Well,' Bonzo added, 'nothing much.'

She tried not to grin as she turned away. 'There now, Mother, can't you see they've not done anything wrong?'

But the old woman had already sensed defeat on that score, and she was looking around sharply for a new line of attack. She darted forward with a speed that took them all by surprise.

'What about this then, Mary?' She had noticed the whistling boy askew on his pedestal. 'They've been interfering with my personal property!'

She began to straighten the boy, but suddenly she lifted him clear and looked at him aghast.

'Look!' She held him out at arm's length. 'Just look what they've done!'

Bonzo knew his mother's good humour could not withstand a fresh onslaught and he acted quickly.

'I can soon rub it off,' he said. 'Look.'

He made a grab for the figure but his grandmother held on. Bonzo's eagerness to put things right made him tug, and her dislike of him made her draw back quickly. There was a small rasping sound as the figure's arm snapped off.

For a long, cold moment there was not a movement in the room. The old woman was pale and had clamped her mouth tight. She gloried in her hatred and in the victory the accident had presented to her.

'I didn't mean it.' Bonzo's voice was very small. The broken arm lay in his hand and he pushed it towards the figure. 'I can fix it. I've got some stuff.'

His mother came forward. 'Let him do it,' she said. 'He's quite good at that sort of thing. And he does like the whistling boy; he's always said so.'

The old woman did not answer. She snatched the broken piece from Bonzo's hand, turned quickly and left the room. His mother, as though she did not know what else to do, had taken out her handkerchief, licked it and was wiping the marks from his face.

She had only just begun when, from the yard at the back, there

134

came a dull crash and then a pounding as something heavy was beaten against the flagstones.

Bonzo's mother kept on wiping until every mark had left his face. Tom was still rubbing at his own skin when the old woman's tread made them stop.

She stood in the doorway.

'You'll have a job to put him together, now, sonny lad,' she said. 'I've taken a hammer to him.'

'Oh, Mother.' The large figure of Bonzo's mother sagged. She spoke quite quietly. 'Why did you have to do that?'

'Because I will not have him touch anything of mine. Nothing. He's just like his father. Useless. Wasting everybody's time.'

'Mother!'

It was almost a wail, but the old woman advanced further into the room, pushing her daughter aside and sat herself heavily in a chair beside the dining table. She was breathing hard and her cheeks were bluish.

'It's no good, Mary. You should never have married that man. You know I never liked him. And now look what's happened. It's all his fault. All of it.'

Bonzo's mother was crying, the tears running gently down her large cheeks.

Bonzo himself was almost in tears, but anger made him shout at his grandmother. 'I hate you!' he yelled. 'Everybody hates you!'

And then he ran, out of the front door into the street.

Tom hesitated, not knowing what to do. Bonzo's mother was silently weeping and the old woman's pinched face was saying bitterly, 'And good riddance. Like father like son. May he never come back.'

And then Tom could stand it no longer. He plunged out of the room and out of the house.

It was not until they had reached the market place that he caught up with Bonzo, and even then Bonzo kept his face turned away. Tom knew he had been crying as he ran.

They wandered aimlessly for a long while before Tom eventually persuaded him to come home to tea, but Bonzo would only do so after he had written a note and Tom had pushed it through the letter box.

'I don't want to worry her,' he said. 'She worries about everything.'

136

Bonzo's own worries hung over him like a cloud all evening. They met the others in the park and, although the afternoon disagreement about cricket had been forgotten, nothing else they did aroused much excitement and as dusk gathered they had been reduced to chasing each other through the shrubbery. Gradually they became widely separated and the game expanded to encompass the entire park. It became good fun to stalk a distant figure, track him down and catch him, and after a while they began to hunt in pairs, calling to each other in barks and yelps as they closed in on their prey.

Tom and Bonzo came together.

'What do you think?' said Tom.

'I saw one over there.' Bonzo pointed towards a group of trees that stood alone in the grass. 'Let's get him.'

He was enjoying himself at last and Tom felt his own heart lift. 'Right,' he said. 'You go that way. Whistle when you're in position.'

They parted, loping across the darkening grass like a pair of wolves. Soon the copse was between them. Tom changed direction and crept towards it. He heard Bonzo's whistle and answered it.

There were five large trees in the copse, standing roughly in a circle. Through them, Tom thought he could see Bonzo in the open on the far side, but he was not sure he could see anybody in the darkness at the centre. He lay full length and looked along the grass. There was a dark shape in the middle. Their victim was simply sitting there, unaware he was trapped.

Bonzo on his side of the trees was crawling forward. He heard Tom's whistle and answered it. The figure crouching in the centre paid no attention. The plan was working perfectly and Bonzo forgot everything else.

Then they were each behind a tree trunk and ready to edge forward. The time for whistling had passed. Tom saw Bonzo come out into the open to begin his final dash and he also lunged from cover.

But suddenly there was nothing to aim for. Their victim had outwitted them. He had gone.

They pulled up short and then, away to one side, as though it had been one of themselves, came a low whistle. They were being mocked.

Together they ran towards the place, but as they did so a figure broke away, ran and twisted and was behind another trunk out of reach. They heard him laugh.

It happened again. Their dash was thwarted. They pulled up together, leaning against a tree, panting.

'Tell you what,' said Bonzo, gasping, 'I'm going to take my shoes and socks off.'

'That's not a bad tell-you-what for once,' said Tom.

Barefoot they ran much faster and quieter. They were very nearly the match for their tormentor who was also unshod and whose shirt, like theirs, hung from his trousers and flapped like rags as he ran.

It became a three-way game. They chased each other, dodging and twisting among the five trees, hiding, giving a clue with a whistle, and then chasing to a new hiding place. It was getting very dark, but still the game went on, fast and furious, making them twist and weave as though in a dance.

Suddenly there was silence. One figure was in the middle again, daring the others. He stood with his hands in his pockets, his bare feet planted firmly in the grass, his head thrown back, and he whistled. The other two crept closer. They could hear each other panting but all they could see was the glimmer of their shirts.

138

They leapt. They grabbed limbs, heaved and rolled in the dust, and then they sat up.

'Got you,' said Tom.

'It's me,' said Bonzo. 'You've got me.'

'Where's the other one, then?'

But he was gone. They searched and called out, but it was too dark to have any hope of finding him. After a while they put on their socks and shoes and wandered out of the park.

'That was good,' said Bonzo. 'I enjoyed that.' As he got closer to home, however, the shadows began to gather again and he fell silent.

'We'll have another game tomorrow night,' said Tom. 'Perhaps he'll be there.'

'Maybe.'

They stood outside Bonzo's door. He was reluctant to go in.

'Don't worry about it,' said Tom. 'She'll have got over it by now.'

They both looked at the window beside the door. Behind the net curtain there should have been the glimmer of the whistling boy's pale face. There was nothing but darkness.

'She broke him up,' said Bonzo. 'There was no need for that.'

The door was suddenly jerked wide. Both of them looked up, their mouths open. Bonzo's mother stood there.

'I heard you talking,' she said. 'Has anybody spoken to you?'

They shook their heads, not understanding. There was something strange about her.

'It's your Granny,' she said. 'She was taken ill just after you left. She's dead.'

They stood there, all three, in the silent street. Tom remembered the blueness in the old woman's face and the catch in her breath after she had broken the whistling boy into pieces. Nobody spoke. And then, from somewhere in the park, the sound reached them. It must have been the boy they had just left. He whistled. He was still there, running barefoot in the dark. They listened. His whistle came once again, and then his laughter from deep among the trees.

JOHN GORDON

The Promise

Trevor was pretty lucky.

His family was rich, they had been builders in his town as far back as anyone could remember. Ever since he was born, Trevor had been given everything a boy could want. He was quite good at school, and was about to go to Cambridge at the end of the summer. He was one of those boys who seemed to be captain of everything. Tennis, rugby, cricket, he was even hard to beat at chess.

He was first choice when party invitations were sent out, and small boys would pretend he was a friend of theirs.

Sometimes, Trevor would take out the prettiest girls, because, when his spots cleared up, he was reasonably good looking.

In fact, Trevor had everything going for him.

In spite of all of this, he was desperately unhappy.

He was afraid of death.

His life held so much promise, he was terrified of ever having to leave it all.

As he grew older, Trevor became more and more cautious. He hated to cross busy roads, because of the traffic. He always wore a scarf, in case he caught a cold that might prove fatal. He had NEVER climbed a tree, and he always avoided dogs, in case they savaged him to death.

Naturally, living the way he did, he missed out on a lot of the fun readily available to most of his friends. At night, Trevor would lie awake, inventing new ways of protecting himself against everything. Ways like taking the wheels off his roller skates, just in case . . . Sleep was not easy for Trevor, and he would lie there in the dark, pleading to anyone up there who might hear him: 'Please, please please, let me live to be a hundred (at least!).'

One night in particular, Trevor was feeling more uneasy than ever. He had been watching television, and on the news there had been an item about a British tourist in Libya who had died from a

camel bite. 'Good heavens,' he groaned to himself, 'that could quite easily happen to me.'

He made a mental vow, NEVER to go to a zoo, or to a circus, or to a pet shop, or to Libya.

And ... he stepped up his pleas in his darkened bedroom, 'PLEASE let me live to be a hundred.'

The answer came as a severe shock. A thin voice, smooth and quiet, came from the gloom at the bottom of his bed:

'If that's what you want, Trevor, I'm sure it can be arranged.'

Trevor sat bolt upright. His first thought was that the owner of the voice might do him some harm. Peering over his duvet, he was able to make out a figure sitting on the end of his bed. A neat, well-dressed figure, with oily hair, and a lily in his lapel.

'Who are YOU?' gurgled Trevor, his nails biting into his palms.

'Oh, Satan, Beelzebub, Lucifer, Mastema, I've lots of names. You can call me Nick. As I was saying, I can quite easily fix it for you to live to be a hundred.'

Happiness swelled up in Trevor, but he was suspicious too.

'I've heard about your way of helping people before,' he muttered, 'you either tell lies, or ask for something nasty in return.'

Nick pulled a Turkish cigarette from a horn case, and put it to his lips where it lit itself. It was so quiet, Trevor could hear the tobacco crackling. Nick's face, lit by the red glow of the cigarette, wore an expression of hurt kindliness.

141

'You shouldn't believe all those old stories about me, my boy, everybody's got me wrong. I NEVER tell lies, and I certainly don't want anything from you in return.'

He drew on his cigarette, almost sadly.

'All I want to do, is to help you. If you want to live to be a hundred, I can fix it for you. No conditions, what do you say?'

'Yes please!' said Trevor.

Nick's face relaxed into a smile. He nodded kindly, and faded into the night.

From that night on, Trevor's life changed. Somehow, he believed Nick's sincerity, 'a sort of Nick'll Fix It', he thought.

All fear of death left him.

That August was spent in Libya, swimming in the Mediterranean. He didn't drown. He even rode on a camel, which turned out to be a gentle creature. The summer passed in carefree happiness, and in due course, Trevor went up to Cambridge.

Naturally he won umpteen blues, and was a hit at the May Ball. His girlfriend was both beautiful and rich, and she drove a Ferrari. Not to be outdone, Trevor bought himself a brand new M.G. Midget. One night, just before Christmas, Trevor was bowling along the Newmarket Road. He had been invited to spend Christmas with Prunella's parents. (Prunella was his girlfriend's name. Everyone except Trevor called her Prune, but that's by the by.)

The night was clear and crisp. In his little sports car, with his college scarf streaming out behind him, Trevor reflected that life was GOOD. What was even better, was that he had eighty years more life in front of him, guaranteed by Nick.

With his mind on his good fortune, and not on the road, Trevor's Christmas ended with a patch of oil lying on the road. Then a bus stop, then a traffic island, then a tree (in the middle of the traffic island. A tall fir tree, covered in fairy lights and imitation presents), then a stone wall.

Trevor didn't even know about the tree or the stone wall.

As the mists cleared, Trevor opened his eyes. He remembered the skid, and he remembered hurtling through the air, yet he felt no pain. It was dark.

He was lying down, he could feel the soft texture of silk. Aware of someone being near him, he tried to sit up, only to bump his head on

142

a sort of roof, or lid. He tried to reach out a hand, but there was no room in the long box. It smelt of earth, and disinfectant.

Squinting towards his feet, he could see Nick, strangely small, and crouching. He was smiling, in the glow of a Turkish cigarette.

Waves of panic swirled over Trevor, quickly turning to anger.

'I'm DEAD,' he screeched at Nick, 'AND BURIED! You said I'd live to be a hundred. You LIED to me!'

Nick looked hurt.

'I told you, I NEVER LIE. The doctors only THOUGHT you were dead, I pulled you through.

     I PROMISED . . .

                        you WILL live to be a hundred.'

Still smiling, Nick left Trevor alone.

TONY ROSS